THE MYSTERY OF THE VANISHED PRINCE

THE MYSTERY SERIES
BY Enid Blyton

Enid Blyton

THE MYSTERY OF THE VANISHED PRINCE

EGMONT

Enid Blyton

EGMONT
We bring stories to life

First published in Great Britain 1951
by Methuen & Co Ltd
This edition published 2013
by Egmont UK Limited
The Yellow Building
1 Nicholas Road
London W11 4AN

ISBN 978 0 6035 6930 2

A CIP catalogue record for this title
is available from the British Library

56917/1

Printed and bound in Great Britain by the CPI Group

CONTENTS

1. WHAT A WASTE OF HOLIDAYS!

'I haven't liked these holidays one bit,' said Bets dolefully to Pip. 'No Larry, no Daisy, no Fatty – a real waste of summer holidays!'

'Well, you've had *me*,' said Pip. 'Haven't I taken you for bike rides and picnics and things?'

'Yes – but only because Mother said you had to,' said Bets, still gloomy. 'I mean – you had to do it because Mother kept saying I'd be lonely. It was nice of you – but I did know you were doing it because it was your duty, or something like that.'

'I think you're very ungrateful,' said Pip, in a huff.

Bets sighed. 'There you are – in a huff again already, Pip! I do wish the others were here. It's the first hols that everyone but us have been away.'

'Well, the other three will be back in a few days'

time,' said Pip. 'We will still have two or three weeks left of these hols.'

'But will there be enough time for a mystery?' asked Bets, rolling over to find a shadier place on the grass. 'We nearly *always* have a mystery to solve in the hols. I haven't always liked our mysteries – but somehow I miss it when we don't have one.'

'Well, find one then,' said Pip. 'What *I* miss most is old Buster.'

'Oh *yes*,' said Bets, thinking of Fatty's joyful, mad little Scottie dog. 'I miss him too. The only person I *keep* seeing that I don't want to see is Mr Goon.'

Mr Goon was the village policeman, a pompous and ponderous fellow, always at war with the five children. Bets seemed to meet him three or four times a day, cycling heavily here and there, ringing his bell violently round every corner.

'Look – there's the postman,' said Pip. 'Go and see if he's got anything for us, Bets. There might be a card from old Fatty.'

Bets got up. It was very hot and although she wore only a sundress of frilly cotton, she still felt as if she was going to melt. She went to meet the postman, who was cycling up the drive.

'Hello postman!' she called. 'I'll take the letters.'

'Right, Missy. Two cards – one for you and one for your brother,' said the postman. 'That's all.'

Bets took them. 'Oh, good!' she said. 'One's from Fatty – and it's for me!'

She ran back to Pip. 'A card for you from Larry and Daisy,' she said, 'and one for me from Fatty. Let's see what they say . . .'

Pip read his card out loud at once. 'Coming back the day after tomorrow, thank goodness. Any mystery turned up? We shan't have much time for one these hols unless we can dig one up quickly! We're very suntanned. You won't know us! Good disguise, of course! See you soon. Love to Bets – Larry and Daisy.'

'Oh *good, good, good*!' said Bets, in delight. 'They'll be round here tomorrow, sure as anything. Now listen to *my* card, Pip.'

She read it out. 'How's things, Bets? I hope you've got a first class mystery for me to set my brains to work on when I return the day after tomorrow. When do Larry and Daisy come back?

It's time the Five Find-Outers (and Dog) got their teeth into something. Be nice to see you again, and old Pip too. Fatty.'

Bets rubbed her hands together in glee. Her face shone. '*All* the Find-Outers will be together tomorrow,' she said. 'And though there's not even the smell of a mystery about, I guess Fatty will run straight into one as soon as he comes.'

'Hope you're right,' said Pip, lying back on the grass again. 'I must say these hols have been pretty boring. I'd like a good thrilling, juicy mystery to end up with.'

'What do you mean – a *juicy* mystery?' said Bets, puzzled.

Pip couldn't be bothered to explain. He lay and thought of all the mysteries he and Bets, Larry and Daisy, Fatty (and Buster, of course) had solved. There was the burning cottage – and the disappearing cat – and the hidden house – gosh, there were a lot!

He suddenly felt hungry for another mystery. He sat up and looked at Bets. 'Let's get the morning paper and see if there's anything thrilling in it,' he said. 'Anything that has happened near us. We could tell Fatty as soon as he comes then, and he might get us all on to it.'

Bets was thrilled. She went to get the paper. She brought it out to Pip and they both studied it carefully. But there didn't seem to be anything happening at all.

'It's nothing but pictures of frightful women and their clothes, and horses racing, and what hot weather it is, and –'

'Cricket scores, and . . .' went on Bets, in a voice as disgusted as Pip's.

'Oh well – cricket scores are *interesting*,' said Pip, at once. 'Look here – see this bowling analysis here?'

Bets wasn't in the least interested in cricket. She turned the page.

'Just like a girl,' said Pip, in an even more disgusted voice. 'The only thing of real importance in the paper is the cricket – and you don't even look at it!'

'Here's something – look, it's something about Peterswood, our village,' said Bets, reading a small paragraph down in a corner. 'And it mentions Marlow too – that's quite near.'

'What is it?' asked Pip, interested. He read the paragraph and snorted. 'Huh – that's not a mystery, or even anything interesting.'

Bets read it out. 'The weather has been very kind to the school camps on the hills between Peterswood and Marlow. This week two or three interesting visitors have joined the camps. One is little Prince Bongawah of Tetarua State who amused everyone by bringing a state umbrella with him. Needless to say he only used it once!'

'Well, if you think that even Fatty can make any mystery or even be *interested* in a silly thing like that, you'd better think again,' said Pip. 'Who cares about Prince Bongabangabing, or whatever his name is?'

'Bongawah,' said Bets. 'Where's Tetarua State, Pip?'

Pip didn't know and didn't care. He rolled over on his front. 'I'm going to sleep,' he said. 'I'm too hot for words. We've had five weeks of hot sun and I'm tired of it. The worst of our weather is that it never stops when it makes up its mind to do something.'

'I don't care about the weather or anything,'

said Bets, happily. 'It can do what it likes now that Fatty and the others are coming back!'

Larry and Daisy came back first. They arrived home the next morning, helped their mother to unpack, and then went straight round to Pip and Bets.

'Larry! Daisy!' shouted Bets joyfully, as they came into the garden. 'I didn't think you'd be back so early. Gosh, how brown you are!'

'Well, you're not so bad either,' said Daisy, giving little Bets a hug. 'It's been ages since we saw each other! Such a waste of hols when we can't go mystery-hunting together!'

'Hello Bets, hello Pip,' said Larry. 'Any news? I must say you're a bad correspondent. I sent you four postcards and you never wrote once!'

'*You* sent them! I like *that*!' said Daisy, indignantly. 'I wrote every single one of them! You never even addressed them.'

'Well, I *bought* them,' said Larry. 'Hey – any news of old Fatty? Is he back yet?'

'Coming today,' said Bets joyfully. 'I keep listening for his bicycle bell, or old Buster's bark. Won't it be lovely for all five of us – and Buster, of course – to be together again!'

Everyone agreed. Bets looked round at the little group, glad to have Larry and Daisy there – but nothing was ever the same without Fatty. Fatty, with his sly humour and enormous cheek and brilliant brains. Bet's heart swelled with joy to think he would soon be there too.

'There's the telephone,' said Pip, as a loud, shrilling ring rang out from the house. 'Hope it's not for me. I feel I simply cannot get up. I think I'm stuck to the grass.'

Mrs Hilton, Pip's mother, appeared at a window. 'That was Frederick on the telephone,' she called. 'He's back home, and will be round to see you very soon. He says, will you please watch out for him, as he's so brown you may not know him. He probably won't know any of *you* either, you're so tanned!'

Everyone sat up straight at this news. 'Oh, I *wish* I'd answered the phone,' said Bets. 'Fatty has such a nice *grinny* voice on the phone.'

Everyone knew what she meant. 'Yes – sort of chortly,' said Larry. 'Gosh, I wish I was always as sure of myself as Fatty is. He never turns a hair.'

'And he *always* knows what to do, whatever happens,' said Bets. 'I say – do you think he'll come in disguise, just for a joke?'

'Yes, of course he will,' said Larry. 'I bet he's got a whole lot of new tricks and disguises and things – and he'll want to practise them on us at once. I know Fatty!'

'Then we'd better look out for someone peculiar,' said Daisy, excited. 'We simply *can't* let him take us in the very first minute he comes back!'

Fatty was, of course, simply marvellous at disguising himself. He could make his plump cheeks even bigger by inserting cheek pads between his gums and his cheek inside his mouth. He had a wonderful array of false teeth that could be fitted neatly over his own. He had shaggy eyebrows to stick over his own modest ones, and any amount of excellent wigs.

In fact, most of his considerable pocket money went on such things, and he was a never-ending source of joy and amusement to the others when he donned one of his many disguises to deceive them or someone else.

'Now we'll watch out,' said Pip. 'Everyone who

comes in at the gate is suspect – man, woman, or child! It *might* be old Fatty!'

They hadn't long to wait. Footsteps could be heard dragging up the drive, and then a large, feathered hat appeared bobbing above the hedge that ran along the pathway to the kitchen entrance. A very brown, plump face looked over the hedge at them, with long gold earrings dangling from the ears, and ringlets of black curls bobbing beneath the dreadful hat.

The children stared. The face smiled and spoke. 'Buy some nice white 'eather? Bring you luck!'

Round the hedge came a large gypsy woman, in a long black skirt, a dirty pink blouse, and a red shawl. Her feathered hat nodded and bounced on her black curls.

'Fatty!' screamed Bets at once, and ran over at top speed. 'Oh, you're Fatty, you are, you are! I recognised your voice – you didn't disguise it enough!'

2. FATTY ARRIVES

The other three children did not call out or run over. This woman seemed much too tall to be Fatty – though he *was* tall now. The gypsy woman drew back a little as Bets came running over, shouting joyfully.

"Ere! 'Oo are you a-calling Fatty?' she said, in a husky voice. 'What you talking about?'

Bets stopped suddenly. She stared at the woman, who stared back insolently, with half-closed eyes. Then the gypsy thrust a bunch of bedraggled heather at Bets, almost into her face. 'Lucky white 'eather,' she whined. 'Buy some, little Missy. I tell you, I ain't sold a spray since yesterday.'

Bets backed away. She looked round at the others. They still sat there, grinning now, because of Bets' sudden fright. She went very red and walked back to the other three children.

The woman followed, shaking her heather in

quite a threatening manner. 'If you don't want my 'eather, you let me read your 'and,' she said. 'It's bad luck to cross a gypsy, you know.'

'Rubbish,' said Larry. 'Go away, please.'

'What do she want to call me Fatty for?' said the woman angrily, pointing at poor Bets. 'I don't reckon on insults from the likes of you, see?'

The cook suddenly appeared, carrying a tray of lemonade for the children. She saw the gypsy woman at once.

'Now you clear off,' she called. 'We've had enough strangers lately at the back door.'

'Buy a spray of 'eather,' whined the woman again and thrust her spray into the cook's angry face.

'Bets – run and fetch your father,' said the cook, and Bets ran. So did the gypsy woman! She disappeared at top speed down the drive and the children saw her big, feathered hat bobbing quickly along the top of the hedge again.

They laughed. 'Gosh,' said Pip, 'just like old Bets to make an idiotic mistake like that. As if anyone could think that awful old creature was Fatty! Though, of course, she did have rather a husky voice for a woman. That's what took Bets in.'

'It nearly took me in too,' said Daisy. 'Hello, here's someone else!'

'Butcher boy,' said Pip, as a boy on a bicycle came whistling up the drive, a joint of meat in his basket on the front.

'It *might* be Fatty,' said Bets, joining them again, looking rather subdued. 'Better have a very good look. He's got a fine butcher boy disguise.'

They all got up and stared hard at the boy who was now standing at the back door. He whistled loudly, and the cook called out to him.

'I'd know it was you anywhere, Tom Lane, with that whistling that goes through my head. Put the meat on the table, will you?'

The four children gazed at the boy's back. He certainly *might* be Fatty with a curly brown wig. Bets craned forward to try and make out if his hair *was* a wig or not. Pip gazed at his feet to see if they were the same size as Fatty's.

The boy swung round, feeling their stares. He screwed up his face at them cheekily. 'Never seen anyone like me before, I suppose?' he said. He turned himself round and round, posing like a model. 'Well, take a good look. Fine specimen of a butcher's boy, I am! Seen enough?'

The others stared helplessly. It *could* be Fatty – it was more or less his figure. The teeth were very rabbitty though. Were they real or part of a disguise?

Pip took a step forward, trying to see. The boy backed away, feeling suddenly half-scared at the earnest gaze of the four children.

'Here! Anything wrong with me?' he said, looking down at himself.

'Is your hair real?' said Bets suddenly, feeling sure it was a wig – and if it was, then the boy must be old Fatty!

The butcher's boy didn't answer. He looked very puzzled, and put up his hand to feel his hair. Then, quite alarmed by the serious faces of the others, he leapt on his bicycle and pedalled fast away down the drive, completely forgetting to whistle.

The four stared after him. 'Well – if it *was* Fatty, it was one up to him,' said Larry, at last. 'I just don't know.'

'Let's have a look at the meat he left on the table,' said Pip. 'Surely even Fatty wouldn't go bicycling about with joints of meat, even if he *was* pretending to be a butcher's boy. Sausages would be much cheaper to get.'

They went into the scullery and examined the meat on the table. The cook came in, astonished to see them bending over the joint.

'Don't tell me you're as hungry as all that,' she said, shooing them away. 'Now don't you start putting your teeth into raw meat, Pip!'

It did look as if Pip was about to bite the meat; he was bending over it carefully to make quite sure it was a real joint, and not one of the many 'properties' that Fatty kept to go with his various disguises. But it was meat all right.

They all went out again, just as they heard a rat-a-tat-tat at the front door. 'That's Fatty!' squealed Bets and rushed round the drive to the front door. A telegram boy stood there with a telegram.

'Fatty!' squealed Bets. Fatty had often used a telegram boy's disguise, and it had been a very useful one. Bets flung her arms round his plump figure.

But, oh dear, when the boy swung round, it certainly was not Fatty. This boy had a small, wizened face, and tiny eyes! Clever as Fatty was at

disguises, he could never make himself like this!
Bets went scarlet.

'I'm so sorry,' she said, backing away. 'I – I
thought you were a friend of mine.'

Her mother was now standing at the open door,
astonished. What was Bets doing, flinging her arms
round the telegram boy? The boy was just as
embarrassed as Bets. He handed in the telegram
without a word.

'Behave yourself, Bets,' said Mrs Hilton, sharply.
'I'm surprised at you. Please don't play silly jokes
like that.'

Bets crept away in shame. The telegram boy
stared after her, amazed. Larry, Pip, and Daisy
laughed till they ached.

'It's all very well to laugh,' said Bets, dolefully. 'I
shall get into an awful row with Mother now. But
honestly, it's exactly like one of Fatty's disguises.'

'Well, of course, if you're going to think every
telegram boy is Fatty, just because Fatty's got a
telegram boy's uniform, we're in for a funny time,'
said Pip. 'Gosh, I wish old Fatty would come. It's
ages since he telephoned. The very next person
must be Fatty!'

It was! He came cycling up the drive, plump as ever, a broad grin on his good-humoured face, and Buster running valiantly beside the pedals!

'Fatty! FATTY!' shrieked everyone, and almost before he could fling his bicycle into the hedge, all four were on him. Buster capered round, mad with excitement, barking without stopping. Fatty was thumped on the shoulder by everyone, and hugged by Bets, and dragged off into the garden.

'Fatty – you've been ages coming!' said Bets. 'We thought you'd be in disguise, and we watched and watched.'

'And Bets made some simply frightful mistakes!' said Pip. 'She's just flung her arms round the telegram boy! He was really startled.'

'He still looked alarmed when I met him cycling out of the gate,' said Fatty, grinning at Bets. 'He kept looking round as if he expected Bets to be after him with a few more hugs.'

'Oh, Fatty, it's great to see you again,' said Bets, happily. 'I don't know *how* I could have thought any of those people here this morning were you – that gypsy woman, the butcher boy, and the telegram boy.'

'We honestly thought you'd be in disguise,' said Larry. 'Gosh, how brown you are. You haven't got any paint on, have you? I've never known you get burnt so brown.'

'No, I'm just myself,' said Fatty modestly. 'No powder, no paint, no false eyelashes, no nothing. I must say you're all pretty brown yourselves.'

'Woof,' said Buster, trying to get on to Bets' knee.

'He says he's sunburnt too,' said Bets, who could always explain what Buster's woofs meant. 'But it doesn't show on him. Darling Buster! We *have* missed you!'

They all settled down to the iced lemonade that was left. Fatty grinned round. Then he made a surprising statement. 'Well, Find-Outers – you're not as smart as I thought you were! You've lost your cunning. You didn't recognise me this morning when I came in disguise!'

They all set down their glasses and stared at him blankly. In disguise? What did he mean?

'What disguise? You're not in disguise,' said Larry. 'What's the joke?'

'No joke,' said Fatty, sipping his lemonade. 'I came here in disguise this morning to test out my faithful troop of detectives, and you didn't recognise your chief. Shame on you! I was a bit afraid of Bets though.'

Pip and Bets ran through the people who had appeared since breakfast that morning. 'Mrs Lacy – no, you weren't her, Fatty. The postman – no, impossible. The man to mend the roof – no, he hadn't a tooth in his head. That old gypsy woman – no, she really was too tall and, anyway, she ran like a hare when she thought I was going to fetch Daddy.'

'The butcher boy – no,' said Larry.

'And we know it wasn't the telegram boy, he had such a wizened face,' said Daisy. 'You're fooling us, Fatty. You haven't been here before this morning. Go on, own up!'

'I'm not fooling,' said Fatty, taking another drink. 'I say, this lemonade is super. I *was* here this morning and I tell you, Bets was the only one I thought was going to see through me.'

They all stared at him disbelievingly. 'Well, who were you then?' said Larry at last.

'The gypsy woman!' said Fatty, with a grin. 'I took you in properly, didn't I?'

'You weren't,' said Daisy, disbelievingly. 'You're pulling our legs. If you'd seen her, you'd know you couldn't be her. Awful creature!'

Fatty put his hand in his pocket and pulled out a pair of long, dangling gilt earrings. He clipped one on each ear. He pulled out a wig of greasy black curls from another pocket and put it on his head. He produced a bedraggled spray of heather and thrust it into Daisy's face.

'Buy a bit of white 'eather!' he said, in a husky voice, and his face suddenly looked exactly like that of the gypsy. The others looked at him silently, really startled. Even without the big feathered hat, the shawl, the basket, and the long black skirt, Fatty was the gypsy woman!

'You're uncanny!' said Daisy, pushing the heather away. 'I feel quite scared of you. One minute you're Fatty, the next you're a gypsy woman. Take that awful wig off!'

Fatty took it off, grinning. 'Believe me now?' he asked. 'Gosh, I nearly twisted my ankle though, when I sprinted down the drive. I honestly thought young Bets here was going to get her father. I wore really high-heeled shoes, and I could hardly run.'

'So that's why you looked so tall,' said Pip. 'Of course, your long skirt hid your feet. Well, you took us in properly. Good old Fatty. Let's drink to his health, Find-Outers!'

They were all solemnly drinking his health in the last of the lemonade when Mrs Hilton appeared. She had heard Fatty's arrival and wanted to welcome him back. Fatty got up politely. He always had excellent manners.

Mrs Hilton put out her hand, and then stared in astonishment at Fatty. 'Well really, Frederick,' she said, 'I cannot approve of your jewellery!'

Bets gave a shriek of delight. 'Fatty! You haven't taken off the earrings!'

Poor Fatty. He dragged them off at once, trying to say something polite and shake hands all at the same time. Bets gazed at him in delight. Good old Fatty – it really was lovely to have him back. Things *always* happened when Fatty was around!

3. DISGUISES

Bets quite expected some adventure or mystery to turn up immediately, now that Fatty was back. She awoke the next morning with a nice, excited feeling, as if something was going to happen.

They were all to meet at Fatty's playroom that morning, which was in a shed at the bottom of his garden. Here he kept many of his disguises and his make-up, and here he also tried out some of his new ideas.

Many a time, the others had arrived at his shed to have the door opened by some frightful old tramp, or grinning errand boy, all teeth and cheeks, or even an old woman in layers and layers of skirts, her cheeks wrinkled, and with one or two teeth missing.

Yes, Fatty could even appear to have a few of his front teeth missing, by carefully blacking out one here and there, so that when he smiled, black gaps appeared, which seemed to be holes where teeth had once been. Bets had been horrified when she had first seen him with, apparently, three front teeth gone!

But this morning, it was Fatty himself who opened the door. The floor was spread with open books. The four children stepped over the madly-barking Buster and looked at them.

'Fingerprints! Questioning of witnesses! Disguises!' said Bets, reading the titles of some of the books. 'Oh, Fatty, is there another mystery on already?'

'No,' said Fatty, shutting the books and putting them neatly into his bookcase at the end of the shed. 'But I seem to have got a bit out of practice since I've been away – I was just testing my brains, you know. Anyone seen old Mr Goon lately?'

Everyone had. They had all bumped into him that morning as they rode round to Fatty's on their bicycles. As usual, the policeman had been ringing his bell so violently that he hadn't heard theirs, and he had ridden right into the middle of them.

'He fell off,' said Daisy. 'I can't imagine why, because none of *us* did. He went an awful bump too, and he was so angry that nobody liked to stop and help him up. He just sat there shouting.'

'Well, he enjoys that,' said Fatty. 'Let's hope he is still sitting there, shouting, then he won't interfere with *us*!'

'Woof,' said Buster, agreeing.

'What are we going to do for the rest of these hols if a mystery doesn't turn up?' asked Pip. 'I mean, we must all have had picnics and outings and things till we're tired of them. And Peterswood is always half-asleep in the summer. Nothing happening at all.'

'We'll have to wind up old Mr Goon then,' said Fatty, and everyone brightened at once. 'Or what about my ringing Inspector Jenks and asking him if he wants a bit of help on anything?'

'Oh, you *couldn't* do that,' said Bets, knowing quite well that Fatty could do anything if he really wanted to. 'Though it would be really nice to see him again.'

Inspector Jenks was their very good friend. He had been pleased with their help in solving many mysteries. But Mr Goon had not been nearly so pleased. The bad-tempered village policeman had wished many a time that the five children and their dog lived hundreds of miles away.

'Well, perhaps I won't bother the Inspector just yet – not till we've smelt out something,' said Fatty. 'But I was thinking we ought to put in a bit of practice at disguises or something like that – we haven't done a thing for weeks and weeks – and suppose something did turn up, we'd make a muddle of it through being out of practice.'

'Oh, *do* let's practise disguises!' said Bets. 'All of us, do you mean?'

'Oh yes,' said Fatty. 'I've got some fantastic new disguises here. I picked them up on my cruise.'

Fatty had been for a long cruise, and had called at many exciting places. He opened a trunk and showed the four children a mass of brilliant-looking clothes.

'I picked these up in Morocco,' he said. 'I went shopping by myself in the native bazaar – my word, things were cheap! I got suits for all of us. I thought they would do for fancy dress, though they will do for foreign disguises too!'

'Oh Fatty – let's try them on!' said Daisy, thrilled. She picked out a bright red skirt of fine silk, patterned in stripes of white.

'There's a white blouse to go with that,' said Fatty, pulling it out. 'Look, it's got red roses embroidered all over it. It will suit you fine, Daisy.'

'What did you get for me, Fatty?' asked Bets, dragging more things out of the trunk. 'You are a most surprising person. You're always doing things nobody else ever thinks of. I'm sure Pip would never bring me home any clothes like this if he went to Morocco.'

'I certainly wouldn't,' said Pip grinning. 'But then, I'm not a millionaire like old Fatty here!'

Fatty certainly seemed to always have plenty of money. He was like a grown-up in that, Bets thought. He seemed to have dozens of rich relations who showered gifts on him. He was always generous with his money though, and ready to share with the rest of them.

Bets had a curious little robe-like dress that reached her ankles. It had to be swathed round and tied with a sash. The others looked at her, and marvelled.

'She looks like a little foreign princess!' said Larry. 'Her face is so sunburnt that she looks like an

Indian – she might *be* an Indian! What a wonderful disguise it would make for her!'

Bets paraded round the shed, enjoying herself. She glanced into the big clear mirror that Fatty kept there, and was startled. She looked like a real little princess! She drew the hood of the dress over her head, and looked round with half-shut eyes. Fatty clapped.

'Very good! An Indian princess! Here Larry – stick this on. And this is for you, Pip.'

The boys pulled on brilliant robes, and Fatty showed them how to wind cloths for bright turbans. All of them seemed to be transformed into a different nationality altogether. Nobody would have thought them English.

Fatty stared at the four parading round his shed. He grinned. His brain set to work to try and evolve a plan to use these bright disguises. A visiting princess? A descent on Mr Goon for some reason? He racked his brains for some bright idea.

'We might be the relations of the little Prince Bongawah of Tetarua State,' said Bets, suddenly. 'I'm sure we look exactly like them!'

'And who's Bongawhatever-it-is when he's

at home?' asked Larry. Bets explained.

'He's a foreign prince who is staying at one of the school camps on the hills between Peterswood and Marlow,' she said. 'We read about him in the paper. He brought a state umbrella with him, but the paper said he only used it once!'

'I bet he did,' said Larry, grinning. 'Got a state umbrella, Fatty?'

'No,' said Fatty, regretfully. He looked at everyone admiringly. 'Honestly, you're wizard! Of course, your suntans make you look first class in those foreign clothes. *Any*one would think you belonged to a different nationality. I only wish you could parade through the village!'

'You dress up too, Fatty, and let's go parading!' said Bets. But Fatty had no time to answer because Buster began to bark loudly, and tore out of the open door at sixty miles an hour.

'Now what's up with *him*?' said Fatty, in surprise. 'I wonder if old Mr Goon's anywhere about?'

Bets peered out of the door and up the garden path. 'It's three boys,' she said. 'Goodness, I know who one is! It's ERN!'

'Ern!' echoed everyone, and ran to the door.

Three boys were coming down the path towards the shed, and Buster was dancing excitedly round Ern's ankles, barking madly.

Fatty shut the door of the shed and faced the others. His eyes sparkled.

'It's Ern Goon!' he said. 'Old Mr Goon's nephew! Let's pretend you're foreign royalty visiting me. If you speak English, speak it badly, see? And if I speak to you in nonsense language, you speak the same. Let's see if we can take old Ern in properly!'

Ern was, as Fatty said, a nephew of Mr Goon the policeman. He had once been to stay with his uncle and had been involved in a mystery. Mr Goon had not been kind to Ern, but the Five Find-Outers had, and Ern thought the world of Fatty. Now here he was, coming to pay a visit with two friends. What a chance to try out the foreign 'disguises'!

Footsteps came right up to the door. Ern's voice could be heard speaking sternly to his two companions. 'Now you behave yourself, see? Both of you. And spit that toffee out, young Sid.'

Whether Sid spat the toffee out or not could not be gathered by the five children in the shed. Bets giggled and Pip gave her a sharp nudge.

There was a knock on the shed door. Fatty opened it and stared solemnly at Ern. Then his face took on a surprised and pleased expression. He smiled broadly and held out his hand.

'Ern! Ern Goon! This *is* a pleasure! Do come in, Ern, and let me introduce you to my foreign visitors!'

4. ERN, SID AND PERCE

Ern was still the same old Ern. He was plump, red-faced, and his eyes bulged slightly, just as his uncle's did, though not quite so much. He grinned shyly at Fatty, and then gazed in awe at the four silent 'foreigners' dressed in such brilliant clothes.

'Pleased to see you, Fatty,' he said, and shook hands for a long time. Then he turned to the two boys behind him. They were not as old as he was, and very alike.

'These here boys are my twin brothers,' he explained. 'This one's Sid – and this one's Perce. Speak up, Sid and Perce. Remember your manners. Come on, say "how do you do" like I told you.'

'How do you do,' said Perce, and bobbed his tousled head, going a brilliant scarlet with his effort at manners.

'Ar,' said Sid, hardly opening his mouth at all. Ern glared at him.

'You still sucking that toffee, Sid? Didn't I tell you to spit it out, see?'

Sid made an agonised face, pointed to his mouth, and shook his head.

''E means, his teeth's stuck fast again,' explained Perce. ''E can't say a word then. Couldn't speak all day yesterday, neither.'

'Dear me,' said Fatty, sympathetically. 'Does he live on toffee then?'

'Ar,' said Sid, with another effort at opening his mouth.

'Does "Ar" mean yes or no?' wondered Fatty. 'But I'm forgetting *my* manners now – Ern, let me introduce you to some very distinguished friends of mine.'

Ern, Sid, and Perce stared unblinkingly at Bets, Pip, Larry, and Daisy, not recognising them in the least as ordinary children. Bets turned her head away, afraid of giggling.

'You have no doubt heard of the little Prince Bongawah of Tetarua State,' went on Fatty. 'This is his sister, Princess Bongawee.' He waved his hand towards the startled Bets.

'Lovaduck!' exclaimed Ern, staring. 'So this is

the Prince's sister, is it? We've seen Prince Bongawah, Fatty – we're camping out in the field next to his. He's a funny little fellow with a cocky little face.' He turned to Sid and Perce.

'You can see they're sister and brother, can't you?' he said, to Bets' indignation. 'Like as two peas!'

'You're right, Ern,' said Perce.

'Ar,' said Sid, working the toffee round a bit to produce his usual remark.

Bets inclined her head majestically and looked at the three awed boys through half-closed lids.

'Popple, dippy, doppy,' she said in a high and mighty voice.

'What's she say?' asked Ern.

'She says, "Your hair is very untidy,"' said Fatty, enjoying himself.

'Coo,' said Ern, and swept his hand over his standing-up hair. 'Well, I didn't know as we were going to see royalty, like, else I'd have done me hair. Who are the others, Fatty?'

'This is Pua-Tua,' said Fatty, waving his hand towards Daisy. 'She is a cousin of the Princess's, and waits on her – a very nice girl indeed.'

Ern bowed, because Daisy did. Perce bowed too,

but Sid didn't. His toffee had got stuck again, and he was concerned with that. His jaws moved unceasingly.

'And the others are Kim-Pippy-Tok, and Kim-Larriana-Tik,' said Fatty, making Bets long to burst into giggles.

Pip moved forward, put his face close to Ern's, and rapidly rubbed noses. Ern started back in surprise.

'It's all right,' said Fatty, soothingly. 'That is their way of greeting a friend.' Sid and Perce backed away, afraid of the same kind of greeting.

'Pleased to meet you,' said Ern, with a gasp. Then he gazed at Fatty in awe. 'You haven't half got some posh friends,' he said. 'What about those other friends of yours – Larry and Daisy and Pip and little Bets?'

'They're not very far away,' said Fatty truthfully. 'Did you say you were camping out somewhere, Ern?'

'Yes,' said Ern. 'We got a chance of a campout, me and Sid and Perce together – got the loan of a tent, see, and Ma said she'd be glad to see the last of us for a bit. So off we skipped, and put up our tent in the field next to one of the school camp fields. We aren't half having a good time.'

'Sright,' said Perce.

'Ar,' said Sid. He suddenly put his hand into his pocket and brought out a round tin. He took off the lid and offered the tin to Fatty. Fatty peered in. It was almost full of dark brown, revolting-looking toffee in great thick pieces.

'Er, no thanks, Sid,' said Fatty. 'I don't want to spoil my dinner. And don't offer it to my visitors, because they will probably have to make speeches this afternoon, and I don't want them to be struck dumb by your toffee.'

'Ar,' said Sid, understandingly, and replaced the lid carefully.

'Where does he get that toffee from?' asked Fatty. 'I've never seen anything like it!'

''E gets it from the 'oopla stall at the Fair near the camp,' explained Perce. ''E's a nib at throwing rings round things, is our Sid. Gets himself a tin of toffee that way each day.'

'Ar,' said Sid, beaming proudly.

'Tickly-pickly-odgery, podgery, pooh,' announced Larry suddenly. Ern, Sid, and Perce stared at him.

'What's 'e say?' asked Perce.

'He says that Sid looks rather like a bit of toffee himself,' said Fatty, at once. 'Chewed-up toffee, he says.'

There was a pause, in which at least five of the children longed to burst into laughter.

'Bit rude that,' said Ern at last. 'Well, I suppose we'd better be off. Been nice to see you, Fatty. Sorry we couldn't see the others too.'

'Have you seen your uncle, Mr Goon?' asked Fatty.

'Coo, no,' said Ern. 'I'd run a mile if I saw him. Don't you remember how he treated me when I stayed with him last year? Sid and Perce don't like him neither. I say, Fatty – any more mysteries going?'

'Not yet,' said Fatty. 'But you never know when one might spring up, do you?'

'Tooky-oola-rickity-wimmy-woo,' said Pip, solemnly. 'We-go-get-icy-cream.'

'Why, he can speak English!' said Ern, in amazement. 'Hear that? I say, why don't we all go and get ice creams? There's a man down by the river we could go to. I don't want to go into the village in case I meet my uncle.'

Fatty grinned. He looked at the other four, who gazed back expectantly. Their 'disguises' had gone down so well with Ern, Sid, and Perce that they were longing to go out in them. Fatty didn't see why they shouldn't! If they took the river road, they wouldn't meet a great many people or attract a crowd, but it would be fun to see the faces of the few they met!

'Iccky, piccky, tominy, wipply-wop, Kim-Pippy-Tok,' he said, politely bowing to Pip, and waving him to the door. 'We'll all go and get ice creams by the river. The Princess must go first, Ern.'

'Course,' said Ern, hurriedly getting out of the way. 'Now *she* would look fine with a state umbrella like her brother had. It'd suit her all right and, what's more, I wouldn't mind carrying it either, she's such a little duck.'

Bets drew her hood over her face to hide her laughter. Fatty looked at Ern as if suddenly struck with a good idea. The others waited expectantly.

'Ah, yes – of course. I'd forgotten that the Princess Bongawee must not go out without her state umbrella,' he said. 'What a good thing you reminded me, Ern.'

'Lovaduck! Has she got one too?' asked Ern.

Fatty disappeared and the others waited. Whatever sort of 'state umbrella' was Fatty going to fetch?

He came back, with an enormous, brightly-coloured umbrella over his head. Actually, it was his mother's golf umbrella, but as Sid, Pearce, and Ern had never seen a golf umbrella in their lives, they honestly thought it was a very grand 'state umbrella'.

'Here, Ern – you can do as you said, if you like, and carry it over the Princess's head,' said Fatty, and Ern nearly had a fit.

'Would she let me?' he asked.

'Dimminy-dooly-tibbly-tok,' said Bets, and gave him a sudden smile. He blushed and looked at Fatty.

'What's she say?' he asked.

'She says, she likes you, and she wants you to carry it for her,' said Fatty promptly.

'The way you understand their language beats me!' said Ern, admiringly. 'But then you always were a one, weren't you, Fatty? Well, I'll be proud to hold the umbrella over Her Highness, or whatever she's called. Sid and Perce, get behind.'

The Five Find-Outers were by now quite unable to contain their laughter. Pip was purple in the face with his efforts to stop exploding. Fatty looked at him.

'Tickly-kickly-koo, jinny-peranha-hook!' he said, and then burst into laughter as if he had made a joke. The others immediately took the opportunity of joining in and Larry, Daisy, Pip, and Bets rocked from side to side, roaring with laughter, holding on to one another, much to the astonishment of Ern and his two brothers.

'What's the joke?' asked Ern, suspiciously.

'It's too difficult to translate it for you,' said Fatty. 'Come on now, the Princess in front, with Ern carrying her umbrella – her cousin, Pua-Tua, just behind – and us following.'

The little procession went down the garden path, passing the kitchen door on the way. The maid stood there, shaking a mat, and she stared open-mouthed as they passed. Ern felt terribly important.

It was very disappointing not to meet more people on the way down to the river. They met old Mrs Winstanton, who was so short-sighted that all she saw was the big umbrella, which made her think it must be raining. She hurried home before she got caught in a shower!

They met the grocer's boy, who stared in amazed and mystified silence. Bets giggled. Ern gave the boy a dignified bow which mystified him still further. What was all this going on? He followed them a little way, and then went to deliver his goods and a tale of 'dressed-up visitors under a HUGE umbrella' to a fascinated housekeeper.

They met nobody else at all. They came to the river path and walked solemnly along it.

'There's the ice cream man!' said Ern, thankfully. 'Pore Sid, he won't be able to have one, what with his toffee and all!'

5. MR. GOON GETS A SURPRISE

The ice cream man was lying on the river bank, fast asleep, his tricycle-van pulled back into the shade. Fatty woke him.

He sat up, amazed at the brilliant group around him, topped by the huge umbrella held by Ern, who was now getting a little tired of its weight.

'What's all this?' said the ice cream man. 'Charades or something?'

Ern opened his mouth to introduce the Princess Bongawee, but Fatty frowned at him. He didn't want the joke to go too far – and he had an uneasy feeling that the ice cream man wouldn't be taken in quite as easily as some people. It wouldn't do to spoil the joke for Ern. Ern, Sid, and Perce were in the seventh heaven of delight to think they had gone walking with a princess and her followers.

'Nine ice creams, please,' said Fatty. Ern corrected him.

'Eight, you mean,' he said.

'You've forgotten Buster,' said Fatty.

'Coo, yes,' said Ern, suddenly remembering that Buster also loved ice cream. Buster had been as good as gold, following the procession solemnly, and hadn't even been to say hello to any dogs he met.

The ice cream man handed out the ice creams, making a few more remarks as he did so.

'Pouring with rain, isn't it?' he said to Ern, who was still valiantly holding the umbrella over Bets. 'Just as well not to get wet.'

'Funny, aren't you?' said Ern.

'Not so funny as you look,' said the ice cream man. 'Where'd you get that umbrella? Out of a cracker?'

'Ha, that's where *you* came from, I spose,' said Ern, at once. 'BANG – and out of a cracker you fell!'

'That's enough, Ern,' said Fatty hastily, seeing a storm about to blow up between the ice cream man and Ern. 'Come on, let's take our ice creams a bit further down the path, where it's cooler.'

The ice cream man remarked that he knew where he could get Ern a clown's hat to go with his umbrella, but Ern was not allowed to reply. Fatty hustled him away, and his umbrella caught in the low-swinging branches of a tree. Bets had to stand still while poor Ern struggled to release it, his ears burning at a few more remarks from the witty ice cream man.

They went on at last again, holding the freezing ice cream cartons in their hands. Sid had one too, and everyone was curious to see how he could manage to eat an ice cream with his mouth still full of toffee. His toffee slab seemed unending. So far as anyone knew, he still had the same piece in his mouth.

And then someone came cycling round the corner of the path – someone burly and red-faced, with a dark blue uniform and helmet!

'It's Uncle!' gasped Ern, in a panic.

'Mr Goon!' said Fatty. 'Old Clear-Orf! Well, well, this is going to be funny!'

Buster recognised Mr Goon with delight. He tore up to his bicycle and jumped at his feet. Goon got off at once and kicked out at the excited little Scottie.

'Clear orf!' he said angrily. 'Here, you, call this dog orf, or I'll push him into the river. Proper little pest, he is.'

'Hello, Mr Goon,' said Fatty, politely. 'I haven't seen you for a very long time. Come here, Buster. Heel, boy, heel!'

Buster ran to Fatty reluctantly, and Mr Goon had time to take in the whole group. He gaped. What a lot of foreigners – and Ern with them. *Ern!* He didn't even know Ern was in the district. He advanced on Ern, who almost dropped the huge umbrella he was still holding.

'ERN! What you doing here?' thundered Mr Goon. 'And bless me, if it isn't Sid and Perce too! What's all this about? And what's the umbrella for?'

'Uncle! Don't shout like that,' begged Ern. 'This is a princess here, and that's why I'm holding an umbrella over her. It's a state umbrella. Don't you know one when you see one?'

Mr Goon didn't even know a golf umbrella when he saw one, much less a state one. He stared at Ern disbelievingly. Ern went on in an urgent voice.

'Uncle, you've heard of Prince Bongawah, who's staying in one of the camps, up on the hills over there, haven't you? Well, this is his sister, Princess Bongawee – and that's her cousin – and . . .'

Goon was amazed. He looked at Bets, wrapped

closely and gracefully in her robes, the hood partly drawn across her sunburnt face. Her face seemed faintly familiar to him, but he didn't for one moment think of Bets Hilton. She stood there rather haughtily, a little scared, without saying a single word.

Goon cleared his throat. He looked at Fatty, who said nothing. 'They were visiting Fatty,' explained Ern. 'And, of course, I told them about Prince Bongawah, who's camping in the field next to us, Uncle – and I'd have known this princess was his sister, they're as alike as two peas.'

'But how did *you* come to be mixed up with them?' asked Goon, suspiciously.

'Your nephew, Ern, came to pay a visit to us, that's all, Mr Goon,' said Fatty, delighted that Ern should be telling Mr Goon such a marvellous tale. 'And the Princess Bongawee liked Ern, and requested him to hold her – er – her state umbrella over her. And Ern's good manners are well-known – so here he is.'

Mr Goon had never had any opinion of Ern's manners at all. He considered that Ern had none. He stared first at Ern, then at the haughty little princess, and then at Fatty. Fatty stared back unwinkingly.

'She a real princess?' asked Mr Goon, in a confidential aside to Fatty. Before Fatty could answer, Bets spoke in a high little insolent voice that amused Fatty immensely.

'Ikky-oola-potty-wickle-tok,' she said.

'What's she say?' asked Goon with interest.

'She wants to know if you're a real policeman,' said Fatty, promptly. 'What shall I tell her?'

Mr Goon glared at him. Bets interrupted again. 'Ribbly-rookatee, paddly-pool,' she said.

'What does *that* mean?' asked Mr Goon. Fatty put on an embarrassed look.

'I don't like to tell you, Mr Goon,' he said.

'Why? What's it matter?' said the policeman, curiously.

'Well, it's rather a personal remark,' said Fatty. 'No, I don't really think I can tell you, Mr Goon.'

'Go on – you tell me,' said Goon, getting angry.

'Yes, you tell him,' said Ern, delighted at the idea of the princess saying something rude about his uncle.

'Ar,' put in Sid, unexpectedly. Goon turned on him at once.

'What you interfering for? And what do you mean by standing there with your mouth full in front of royalty? Go and empty your mouth!'

'Ar,' said Sid, in panic.

'It's toffee, Uncle,' said Ern. 'Stick-me-tight toffee. It can't be spat out.'

Bets went off into a peal of laughter. Then she hurriedly spoke a few more words. 'Wonge-bonga-smelly-fiddly-tok.'

'There she goes again,' said poor Goon. 'You tell me what she said then, Frederick.'

'I couldn't possibly,' persisted Fatty, making Goon feel so curious that he could hardly contain himself. His face began to go purple, and his eyes bulged a little. He stared at the little princess, who giggled again.

'I only say, why he got FROG face!' said Bets, in a very foreign voice. Everyone immediately exploded, with the exception of poor Sid who couldn't get his mouth open.

Mr Goon exploded too, but in a different way. He was very angry. He took a step forward and Ern instinctively lowered the umbrella and put its vast circle just in front of Mr Goon's nose.

'Don't you hurt the princess, Uncle,' came Ern's quavering voice from behind the huge umbrella. Then Buster joined in the fun again, and flew at Mr Goon's ankles, snapping very deftly at the bicycle clips that held his trousers tightly round his legs.

Mr Goon roared in anger. 'I'll report that dog! I'll report you too, Ern – trying to stick that umbrella into me!'

'Mr Goon, I hope you won't upset the relations of the British with the Tetaruans,' said Fatty, solemnly. 'We don't want the Prince of Tetarua complaining that you have frightened his sister. After all, Tetarua is a friendly state. If the Prime Minister had an incident like this reported to him by an angry prince, there might be . . .'

Mr Goon didn't stay to listen to any more. He knew when he was defeated. He didn't know anything about the Tetaruans, but he did know that little states were very touchy nowadays, and he was rather horrified to hear what Fatty said. He got on his bicycle and sailed away in purple dignity.

'I'll have something more to say to you, young Ern,' he shouted, as he pedalled past, with Buster at his back wheel, making him wobble almost into the river. 'I'll come up to your camp, you see if I don't!'

He left Ern petrified by his threat, but still valiantly holding the umbrella. Everyone collapsed weakly on the grass, and even Sid managed to open his mouth wide enough to let out a sudden guffaw.

'Our poor ice creams,' said Bets, suddenly relapsing into English, and looking at the ice cream in her carton. It was like custard. Nobody noticed she was speaking English except Fatty, who gave her a little frown.

They licked up their ice creams with difficulty. Sid managed to pour his somehow into his mouth, between his stuck teeth. Fatty grinned round.

'A most creditable performance!' he said. 'Princess, my congratulations!'

'Binga-bonga-banga,' said Bets, graciously.

'What about fresh ice creams?' said Fatty. But Ern, Perce, and Sid couldn't stay. Ern had heard the church clock striking twelve, and as he had been promised a camp dinner by the caravanners next to his tent if he got back at half past twelve, he felt impelled to go.

He bowed most politely to Bets, and handed the

state umbrella to Fatty. 'Pleased to have met you,' said Ern. 'I'll tell your brother about you when next I see him over the hedge. Like as peas in a pod, you are!'

Sid and Perce nodded a good-bye, and then they all went off to get the ferry across the river to the hills on the other side.

'Thank goodness we can talk properly again,' said Larry. 'My word, Fatty – what a morning! I don't know when I've enjoyed myself so much!'

6. DISAPPEARANCE

Two days later, Fatty, Larry, and Pip all had tremendous shocks. Fatty got down to breakfast before his mother and father, and poured himself some coffee. He took the two papers they had each morning to his own place, and prepared to enjoy them in peace.

The headlines flared at him, big and black. 'Disappearance of a Prince from Camp. Vanishes in the night. Prince Bongawah gone.'

And in Larry's house, Larry too was reading the same headlines out to Daisy, having found the papers on the front doorstep and brought them in.

In Pip's house, Pip was, as usual, trying to read his father's newspaper back to front. The back page was never very interesting to Pip, because it was all about horse-racing, golf, and tennis – none of which he took any interest. Cricket scores were usually in too small print for him to see. So he waited patiently for his father to study the cricket scores himself on the back page, when Pip would be able to read the front page.

And there, staring at him, were some very interesting headlines. 'Prince vanishes. Tetarua informed. Boys in camp questioned.'

Pip nudged Bets and nodded his head towards the paper. She read the headlines too. Good gracious! That must be the Prince Bongawah whose sister she had pretended to be. How very extraordinary! Bets thought hard about it. Would it matter her having pretended? No, it couldn't. They had only done it to play a trick on Ern.

Yet another person was most interested in the disappearance of the young prince. That was Mr Goon, of course. He also read it in his morning newspaper, and a few minutes later, his telephone rang and he had the news from headquarters. He thought rapidly.

My word – I've met the prince's sister, he thought. If we get hold of her, we might get some news! I'd better get on to the Inspector straightaway.

He corrected himself. 'I should say the *Chief* Inspector! He's had a promotion again. I've never had any. Got enemies, I have, no doubt of that. Keeping a good man down, that's what they are. Wait till I get them!'

He brooded for a few minutes on enemies that prevented promotion, and then rang up head-quarters again and asked for the Chief Inspector.

'He's busy,' said the voice at the other end. 'What do you want him for, Goon?'

'Something to do with the Prince Bongawah disappearance,' said Goon, pompously. 'Very interesting.'

'Right. Hold on a minute,' said the voice. Then Goon heard the Chief Inspector's voice – sharp, confident, and a little annoyed.

'What is it, Goon? I'm busy.'

'Sir, it's about that Prince Bongawah, or whatever his name is,' said Goon. 'I've met his sister, sir, the little Princess Bongawee. I wondered if anyone had thought of questioning her. She might know something about her brother's disappearance.'

There was a moment's silence. Then the Chief Inspector's voice came again, sounding astonished.

'Sister? What sister? This is the first time I've

heard of her.'

Goon swelled with importance. 'Yes, sir. I met her two days ago, sir, with her cousin, who looks after her. And two of her train, sir, all very posh and high and mighty.'

There was another astonished pause. 'Is that really you speaking, Goon?' said the Chief Inspector's voice at last. 'This really is so astonishing.'

'Course it's me speaking, sir,' said Goon, surprised and hurt. 'Why shouldn't it be? I'm just reporting something to you, as is my duty. Would you care for me to interview the princess, sir?'

'Wait a minute, wait a minute,' said the Chief Inspector. 'I must ask a few questions of somebody here. We've had no reports of any sister or princess or cousin! I must find out why.'

Goon waited, feeling pleased to have caused such a commotion. Ha – let Chief Inspector Jenks ask all the questions he liked, he'd have to let him, Goon, handle this in the end! That was a bit of luck meeting Fatty with those Tetaruans and their umbrella. A thought struck him. How was it that *Fatty* knew them?

Drat that boy! thought poor Goon. Here I've got

a fine bit of investigation in my hand – and I've got to say it's that big boy who introduced me to the princess! Then the Chief Inspector will get on to that toad of a boy, and he'll take the whole matter out of my hands!

He sat and brooded about this, the telephone receiver stuck to his left ear. Then he brightened. He could say that his nephew, Ern, had introduced him. After all, it *was* Ern who had given him all the details. That was quite true. He needn't bring Fatty into it at all.

The Chief Inspector's voice came down the telephone again, making Goon jump.

'Are you there, Goon? Well, I've made a few enquiries this end, and nobody seems to know anything about a sister who's called Princess Bongawee. But seeing that you appear to have met her, I suppose we must enquire into it. How did you meet her?'

'Well, sir – my nephew Ern was with her, and he told me about her and who she was,' said Goon.

'*Ern* – your nephew *Ern*!' said the Chief Inspector, astounded. He remembered the plump, rather spotty, extremely plain nephew of Mr Goon quite clearly. Hadn't he been mixed up in another mystery? Oh yes – and had come quite well out of it too, in the end. But *Ern*! In the company of a Tetaruan princess! The Chief Inspector wondered again if this telephone call was a hoax. But, no, it couldn't be. He knew that harsh voice of Mr Goon's only too well!

'What was Ern doing with the princess?' asked the Chief Inspector, at last.

'Well – he was holding a – a state umbrella over her,' said Mr Goon, beginning to feel that this tale of his didn't really sound very credible.

There was another pause. The Chief Inspector swallowed once or twice. Was Goon all right? Had he got a touch of the sun? This tale of a princess – and Ern – and a state umbrella sounded nonsense to him. The Chief Inspector simply didn't know what to make of it at all.

'Look here, Goon,' he said, 'this is all very extraordinary, but I suppose there may be something in it if you think it's important enough to telephone me about it. I think I will leave you to contact this – er – princess, and ask her a few questions. Why she's here, when she came, what she's doing, who she's with, and so on. Go and do that now. I'll send a man over to check what you find.'

'Right sir, thank you, sir,' said Goon, pleased that he was going to handle the matter first. He clicked down the receiver, and went to get his helmet. It was a great pity he had to go and see that toad of a boy, Fatty. Frederick Trotteville. Huh! He'd soon show him he'd got to answer his questions though. He'd stand no nonsense from that pest.

He cycled round to Fatty's house. He knocked sharply at the front door. The maid opened it, and he asked for Fatty.

'He's gone out, sir,' said the maid.

'Where's he gone?' demanded Mr Goon.

Mrs Trotteville, Fatty's mother, heard Mr Goon's rather loud voice, and came into the hall.

'Oh, it's you, Mr Goon,' she said politely. 'Did you want Frederick? He's out, I'm afraid. Was there something you wanted to ask him?'

'Well, madam, I did want to ask him a few questions about the Princess Bongawee,' said Mr Goon. 'But perhaps you can tell me. Was she staying here?'

Mrs Trotteville looked amazed. '*What* princess?' she asked. 'I've never even heard of her.'

'She's the sister of that Prince Bongawah that's vanished,' explained Mr Goon.

This didn't convey anything to Mrs Trotteville at all. She hadn't taken any interest in the morning's report of the prince's disappearance. She had merely thought he hadn't liked cold baths or something, and had run away. And anyway, what was it to do with Frederick?

'I'm afraid I can't help you, Mr Goon,' she said. 'Frederick has only been back home for two or three days and, as far as I know, he hasn't been about with any princesses at all. I feel sure he would have introduced them to me if he knew any. Good morning.'

'But – do you mean to say you didn't ask her in to tea or anything?' said Mr Goon desperately.

'Why should I, if I have never even met her?' said Mrs Trotteville, thinking that Mr Goon must be out of his mind. 'Good morning.'

She shut the door and left a perspiring Mr Goon outside. Now he had got to go and find that boy. Where would he be? He might be round at those precious friends of his – the Hilton's – or those other's – Larry and Daisy somebody-or-other.

Mr Goon cycled first to Larry's house. But again he drew a blank. Larry and Daisy were both out.

'Probably round at Frederick Trotteville's,' said their maid. But Mr Goon knew better. Nobody was going to send him trapesing back there again!

He cycled, very red in the face now, down the road, and all the way to Pip's. He cycled up to the front door, and hammered angrily on the knocker.

The five children were out in the garden with Buster. Buster growled at the knocking and Fatty put a restraining hand on him.

Bets went peeping round the hedge to see who it was at the front door. She ran back, looking scared.

'It's Mr Goon. Old Clear-Orf. He looks very red and cross,' she said. 'Oh dear – do you think he's come to ask us about the princess I pretended to be? He's really so very silly, I'm sure he thinks I was real!'

Fatty got up. 'Come along,' he said. 'Out of the gate at the bottom of the garden we go, top speed. If anyone calls us, we're not here. If Goon is hunting for the Princess Bongawee, let him hunt! Do him good. Shut up, Buster – if you bark, you'll give the game away!'

They all fled silently down the garden to the little gate that opened onto the lane at the bottom. Buster ran too, without even half a growl. Something was up, was it? Well, he could play his part too, then!

When Mrs Hilton took Mr Goon out into the garden to find the children, there was no one there. No one in the summer-house either! How peculiar!

'I am *sure* I heard them out here a minute ago,' she said. 'Pip! Bets! Where are you?'

No answer at all. Mrs Hilton called once more and then turned to the purple Mr Goon. 'I expect you will find them either at Frederick Trotteville's, or at Larry's,' she said. 'Perhaps you would like to go there.'

Mr Goon had a vision of himself chasing from one house to another, endlessly in search of an elusive Fatty. He scowled, and sailed away morosely on his bicycle.

'Really,' thought Mrs Hilton, 'that policeman's manners get worse and worse every day!'

7. ERN AND MR GOON

Somebody else was also very excited that morning, besides the Find-Outers and Mr Goon. Ern was most astonished when he heard the news of Prince Bongawah's disappearance. He learnt it in rather a peculiar fashion.

Ever since he had met the Princess Bongawee at Fatty's house, he had kept a lookout for the little prince over the hedge. He was longing to tell him that he had met his sister.

But, somehow, he hadn't caught sight of him. Still, Ern didn't give up, and that very morning he had squirmed right through the hedge, hoping to find the prince himself.

He was most astonished to find two policemen nearby. They pounced on Ern at once. 'What are you doing in this field?' demanded one, his hand on Ern's neck.

'I only just came over to look for someone,' said

Ern wriggling. 'Lemme go. You're hurting.'

'You'll get hurt a lot more if you come interfering here now,' said the policeman grimly. 'You might even disappear – like the little prince!'

This was the first Ern had heard of any disappearance. He stared at the two policemen. 'Has he disappeared?' he said, astonished. 'Coo, think of that! When did he go?'

'Sometime in the night,' said the policeman, watching Ern closely. 'Hear anything? You're camping in that tent, I suppose?'

'Yes. I didn't hear nothing at all,' said Ern at once. 'Coo – to think I met his sister, the princess, a few days ago!'

'Oh yes?' said one of the policemen, mockingly. 'And did you have tea with his mother, the Queen, and dinner with his old man?'

'No. But I had an ice cream with his sister,' protested Ern.

'Oh yes?' said both policemen at once. One of them gave him such a violent shake that Ern almost fell over. 'Now you get along,' he said. 'And just remember, it's always best to keep your nose out of trouble. You and your tales!'

Ern squeezed back through the hole in the hedge, hurt to think that his tale had been disbelieved. He was determined to go and tell Fatty about the prince's disappearance. It didn't occur to him that it was already in all the papers.

He set off by himself, without Sid or Perce. Perce was in a bad temper that morning, and Sid as usual had his mouth full of stick-me-tight toffee, so there was no conversation to be got out of him at all. Ern felt that he wanted a little intelligent company. Neither Sid nor Perce could be called really interesting companions.

He decided to borrow a bicycle from one of the nearby caravanners. There was one there, leaning against the caravan. Ern snooped round, looking for the owner.

He found him at last, a boy a bit older than himself. 'Lend me your bike?' called Ern.

'Cost you,' called back the thrifty owner. Ern parted reluctantly with some money and rode off down the field path to the gate, wobbling over the ruts.

Meanwhile, Mr Goon was cycling grumpily back home again. Just as he turned a corner, he caught sight of a plump boy cycling towards him. It was Ern. Ern, however, was not particularly anxious to meet his uncle, so he turned his bike round hurriedly and made off in the opposite direction.

For some reason, Mr Goon took it into his head to think that the boy in the distance was Fatty in one of his errand boy disguises.

He began to pedal furiously. Oho! So that toad of a boy was up to his tricks again, was he? He was disguising himself so as to keep away from Mr Goon and his questions, was he? Well, he, Mr Goon, would soon put an end to that! He would cycle after him till he caught him.

So Mr Goon cycled. The pedals went up and down furiously, he rang his bell furiously as he rounded the corner, and he looked furious too. Anyone looking at Mr Goon at that moment would have thought that he was on very important business indeed.

Ern took a look over his shoulder when he heard the furious ringing of Mr Goon's bell coming round the corner. He was horrified to find his uncle racing after him down the street. Ern began to pedal very quickly indeed.

'Hey you!' came a loud voice from halfway down the street. Ern's heart almost failed him. His uncle sounded so very stern. But what had he, Ern, done now? Was his uncle going to scold him for protecting the princess with the state umbrella?

Ern pedalled away and shot round a corner. So did Mr Goon. Both got hotter and hotter, and Ern became more and more panic-stricken. Mr Goon began to get very angry indeed. He was absolutely certain it was Fatty leading him this dance. Wait till he got him! He'd pull off his wig, and show him he couldn't deceive him!

Ern turned another corner, and found himself cycling up a path into a barn. He couldn't stop. Hens and ducks fled out of his way. Ern ended up on the floor of a dark barn, panting, and almost in tears.

Mr Goon came up the path at top speed too. He also landed in the dark barn, but not on the floor. He came to a stop just by Ern.

'Now, you just take off that wig,' commanded Mr Goon, in an awful voice. 'And let me tell you what I think of boys who lead me a dance like this, just when they know I want evidence regarding the Princess Bongawee!'

Ern stared up at his uncle in amazement. What was he talking about? Did he think Ern was wearing a wig? It was dark in the barn, and at first Mr Goon did not see that it was Ern. Then, as his eyes grew used to the shadows, he saw who it was. His eyes bulged almost out of his head.

'ERN! What are you doing here?' he almost yelled.

'Well, Uncle – you chased me, didn't you?' said Ern, in alarm. 'I was frightened. Didn't you know it was me? You pedalled after me all right.'

Mr Goon collected himself with an effort. He stared down at Ern, who was still on the floor. 'What did you run away from me for?' he asked sternly.

'I told you. You chased me,' said Ern.

'I chased you because you were running away,' said Mr Goon, majestically.

'Well, Uncle – I ran away because you were chasing me,' said poor Ern again.

'You being cheeky?' asked Mr Goon, in an awful voice.

'No, Uncle,' said Ern, thinking it was time he got

up. He was too much at Mr Goon's mercy on the floor. Anything might happen to him with his uncle so furious! Ern didn't know what was the matter at all. All he had done was to try to get away from his uncle.

'Have you seen that big boy today?' asked Mr Goon, watching Ern slowly and cautiously get up.

'No, Uncle,' said Ern.

'You seen that there princess again?' asked his uncle.

'No, Uncle,' said Ern, in alarm. 'I say – you're not after *her*, are you?'

'Do you know where she lives?' said Mr Goon, thinking that perhaps he might get something out of Ern, if he couldn't find the elusive Fatty.

'Why don't you ask Fatty?' said Ern, innocently. 'He knows her very well. I expect she sees him every day. Coo – she might know something about her brother's disappearance. I never thought of that!'

'Now you listen here, Ern,' said Mr Goon, solemnly. 'You remember Chief Inspector Jenks? Well, I've been talking to him on the phone today, see, about this same disappearance. And he's put me in charge of the case. I'm trying to find that princess to question her. But do you think I can find that pest of a boy to ask him about her? He's nowhere to be found! Makes me think *he's* disappearing too – on purpose!'

Ern picked up his bike, listening hard. He thought it very likely indeed that Fatty was avoiding Mr Goon. Ern considered it was a very sensible thing to do. Perhaps Fatty was on to this case too? Perhaps – oh joy – perhaps a mystery had suddenly turned up right under his very nose? Maybe Fatty was avoiding Mr Goon so that he wouldn't have to give away what he knew about the princess.

Ern grinned suddenly, much to his uncle's astonishment. 'What you grinning at all of a sudden?' he asked suspiciously.

Ern didn't answer. His grin faded. 'Now you look here, young Ern,' boomed Mr Goon, 'if I catch you hanging round Peterswood, hobnobbing with that pest of a boy, I'll have you and Sid and Perce cleared out of that camp in double-quick time – do you hear me? You don't know nothing about this case at all, and you aren't going to know anything, either. I know you and your ways – telling tales of this and that and the other! All you can tell that boy this time is that I'm in charge of this, and if he doesn't tell me all he knows about that princess before teatime, so's I can report to the Chief Inspector, he'll get into serious trouble. Very serious trouble.'

Mr Goon was quite out of breath after this long speech. Ern edged out of the barn. The hens peeping round the door scattered at once, clucking. Ern leapt on his bicycle and rode out at top speed.

'You go and tell that boy I want him!' yelled Mr Goon, as a parting shot. 'I'm not going all over the place after him again!'

Ern cycled quickly to Fatty's, relieved to have got away from his uncle without too much trouble. He hoped to goodness he would find Fatty at home. He was lucky! Fatty was in his shed with the others, keeping a watch for Goon.

Ern poured out his tale, and was disappointed to find that the others already knew about the prince's disappearance from the papers. 'What about that princess, Fatty?' said Ern. 'Don't she know nothing about her brother?'

'Ern – she wasn't a real princess,' said Fatty, thinking it was time to own up to their joke. 'That was only young Bets here dressed up in some things I brought from Morocco. And her cousin was Daisy, and the others were Larry and Pip!'

'Kim-*Larri*ana-Tik, at your service,' said Larry, with a bow.

'Kim-*Pip*py-Tok,' said Pip, with another bow. Ern stared, bewildered. He rubbed his hand over his eyes. He stared again.

'Lovaduck!' he said at last. 'No, I can't believe it! Just you dressed up, little Bets! And you looked a real princess too. Coo! No wonder my uncle's wanting to see you, Fatty, and ask about the princess – and no wonder you don't want to see *him*! Took him in properly, we did! Me with the state umbrella and all!'

Bets began to laugh. 'You were fine, Ern,' she said. 'Oh dear – didn't we talk a foreign language beautifully! Onna-matta-tickly-pop!'

'Beats me how you can talk like that,' said Ern, wonderingly. 'But I say – what's the Chief

Inspector going to say about all this? My uncle says he told him all about the princess this morning, and he's been put in charge of the case! He says I'm to tell you to keep off! *He's* met the princess too, he says, and you've got to tell him where she lives so that he can interview her.

Fatty groaned. 'I knew this would happen! Why did I do such a fool thing! It was just because you turned up when you did, Ern. Well – I suppose I'd better ring up the Chief Inspector and tell him everything. All I hope is that he'll laugh.'

'Better go and do it now,' said Pip, nervously. 'We don't want old Mr Goon round complaining about us again. If you get the Chief Inspector on your side, we'll be all right.'

'Right,' said Fatty, getting up. 'I'll go now. So long! If I'm not back in five minutes, you'll know the Chief Inspector has gobbled me up!'

He went off down the garden path to the house. The others looked rather solemnly at one another. What in the world would the Chief Inspector say when he heard there was no princess?

And worse still – whatever would *Mr Goon* say?

He must have told the Chief Inspector all about her. He wouldn't like it one little bit when he knew it was all a joke!

8. TWO UNPLEASANT TALKS

The Chief Inspector was not at all pleased with Fatty's tale. At first, he couldn't make head or tail of it, and his voice became quite sharp.

'First Goon telephones a cock-and-bull story of some princess who says she's Prince Bongawah's sister, and now you ring me and say there's no such person, it was only Bets dressed up,' said Chief Inspector Jenks. 'This won't do, Frederick. A joke's a joke, but it seems to me you've gone rather far this time. You've made Goon waste time on a lot of nonsense, when he might have been doing a bit of more useful investigation.'

'I quite see that, sir,' said poor Fatty. 'But actually it was all an accident – we'd no idea when we dressed up and called Bets the Princess Bongawee that Prince Bongawah was going to disappear. It was a most unfortunate coincidence. I mean, we couldn't possibly have guessed that was going to happen.'

'Quite,' said the Chief Inspector. 'You have a very curious knack of turning up in the middle of things, Frederick, haven't you? Accidental or otherwise. You'll certainly make Goon gnash his teeth over this! By the way, how on earth did that nephew of his – Ern, or some such name – come to be mixed up in this idiotic princess affair?'

'He just happened to barge in on us when we were dressing up,' explained Fatty. 'You know he and his twin brothers are camping in the field next to where the little prince was camping, don't you? It's a pity he's such an idiot or he might have noticed something.'

There was a pause. 'Yes,' came the Chief Inspector's voice, at last. 'I'd let Goon question them, but I don't think he'd get much out of Ern, somehow. You'd better see if you can find out something, Frederick – though you don't deserve to come in on this, you know, after your asinine behaviour.'

'No, sir,' said Fatty humbly, his face one huge grin at the thought of 'coming in on this'! That meant a little detective work again. Aha! So these hols were going to have something exciting, after all!

'All right,' said Chief Inspector Jenks. 'Make your peace with Goon if you can, and tell him to telephone me afterwards. He will *not* be pleased with you, Frederick. Neither am I. You'd better try and rub off this black mark quickly!'

Without saying good-bye, the Chief Inspector rang off, and Fatty heard the receiver click back into place. He put back his own, and stood by the wall, thinking hard. He felt thrilled, but rather uncomfortable. Quite by accident, he had got mixed up with the Prince Bongawah, simply because Bets had dressed up as a princess and Ern had seen her! How could he have known the prince was going to disappear, and that old Mr Goon would immediately spread the news about his mythical sister? Just like Goon! Always on to the wrong thing!

It was going to be most unpleasant breaking the news to Mr Goon that the Princess of Bongawah was just a joke. She didn't really exist. It was only Bets, dressed up, who had taken in old Mr Goon!

I play too many jokes, thought Fatty to himself. But it's going to be a pretty poor life for me and the others if I cut out all the tricks and jokes we like. We play them too well, I suppose. Gosh – there's Mr Goon coming in at the front gate! Now for it!'

Fatty went to the front door before Mr Goon could hammer at the knocker. He wasn't particularly anxious for his mother to hear what he had to say to Goon.

Goon stared at Fatty as if he couldn't believe his eyes. 'Here I've been chasing you all day and you come and open the door to me before I've even knocked!' he said. 'Where have you been?'

'That doesn't matter,' said Fatty. 'Come into this room, Mr Goon. I've something to say to you.'

He took the burly policeman into the little study, and Goon sat down in a chair, feeling rather astonished. 'I've got plenty to ask *you*,' he began. 'Been after you all day to get some information.'

'Yes. Well, you're going to have quite a lot of information,' said Fatty. 'And I'm afraid it will be a bit of a shock to you, Mr Goon. There's been an unfortunate misunderstanding.'

'Huh!' said Mr Goon, annoyed at Fatty's way of speaking. 'I don't want to know about unfortunate misunderstandings, whatever they may be – I just want to ask you about this here Princess Bonga – er, Bonga-what's-her-name.'

'Bongawee,' said Fatty, politely. 'I was going to tell you about her. She doesn't exist.'

Goon didn't take this in at all. He stared at Fatty, bewildered. Then he poked a big fat finger into the boy's face.

'Now you look here – you can pretend all you like that she doesn't exist, but I saw her with my own eyes. She's important in this here case, see? You may want to pretend that you don't know her now, nor where she is, but I'm not having any of that. I'm in charge of this, and I'm going to demand answers to my questions. Where's this princess now?'

Fatty hesitated. 'Well, I've already told you she doesn't exist,' he said. 'There's no such princess. It was only Bets dressed up.'

Goon went a dull red, and his eyes bulged a little more. He pursed up his mouth and glared. *Now* what was this boy up to? The princess was Bets dressed up! What nonsense! Hadn't he heard her talk a foreign language with his own ears?

'You're making up a tale for some reason of

your own, Frederick,' he burst out at last. 'I not only saw the princess, but I heard her. She talked all foreign. Nobody can talk foreign if they don't know the language.'

'Oh yes, they can,' said Fatty. 'I can "talk foreign" for half an hour if you want me to. Listen!'

He poured out a string of idiotic, completely unintelligible words that left Mr Goon in a whirl. He blinked. How did this boy do these things?

'There you are,' said Fatty, at last. 'Easy! You try, Mr Goon. All you have to do is to let your tongue go loose, if you know what I mean, and jabber at top speed. It doesn't *mean* anything. It's just complete nonsense. You try.'

Mr Goon didn't even begin to try. Let his tongue go loose? Not in front of Fatty, anyway! He might try it when he was by himself, perhaps. In fact, it might be a good idea. He, too, might be able to 'talk foreign' whenever he pleased. Mr Goon made a mental note to try it out sometime when he was quite by himself.

'See?' said Fatty, to the dumbstruck policeman. 'I only just let my tongue go loose, Mr Goon. Do try. Anyway, that's what Bets and the others did

– we didn't really "talk foreign", as you call it.'

'Do you mean to say that that procession Ern was with was just Bets and your friends dressed up?' said poor Mr Goon, finding his tongue at last. 'What about the state umbrella?'

Fatty had the grace to blush. 'Oh that – well, actually it was a golf umbrella belonging to my mother,' he said. 'I tell you, it was all a joke, Mr Goon. Ern happened to come along when they were all dressed up, and you know what he is – he just fell for everything, and swallowed the whole tale of princess and lady-in-waiting and all! We went out for ice creams – and then we met *you*!'

Mr Goon suddenly saw it all now. He was full of dismay and horror. To think of all he had told the Chief Inspector too! How was he to get out of *that*? He buried his face in his hands and groaned, quite forgetting that Fatty was still there.

Fatty felt extremely uncomfortable. He didn't like Mr Goon at all, but he hadn't meant to get him into this humiliating fix. He spoke again.

'Mr Goon, it was a silly mistake and most unfortunate, of course, that the Prince Bongawah should go and disappear just after we'd pretended

Bets was his sister. I've told the Chief Inspector all about it. He's just as annoyed with me as you are, but he does see that it was pure coincidence – just an unlucky chance. We're all very sorry.'

Mr Goon groaned again. 'That golf umbrella! I told him it was a state umbrella. He'll think I'm potty. Everyone will think I'm potty. Here I am, struggling for promotion, doing my very best, and every time you come along and upset the apple cart. You're a toad of a boy, that's what you are!'

'Mr Goon, I *am* sorry about this,' said Fatty. 'Look here – let's work together this time. I'll try and make up for this silly beginning. We'll solve this mystery together. Come on – be a sport!'

'I wouldn't work with you if the Chief Inspector himself told me to!' said Mr Goon, rising heavily to his feet. 'Once a toad, always a toad! And what would working with you mean? *I'll* tell you! False clues put under my nose! Me running about at night to find people that aren't there! Me arresting the wrong person while you've got the right one up your sleeve! Ho – *that's* what working with you would mean!'

'All right,' said Fatty, getting angry at being

called a toad so often. 'Don't work with me then. But if I can put any information your way I will, all the same – just to make up for upsetting your apple cart.'

'Gah!' said Goon, stalking out. 'Think I'd listen to any information from you! You think again, Frederick Trotteville. And keep out of this. I'm in charge, see, and I'll solve this mystery, or my name's not Theophilus Goon!'

9. A LITTLE 'PORTRY'

Mr Goon went to telephone the Chief Inspector. He felt extremely gloomy and downhearted. Why did he always believe everything Fatty said and did? Why didn't he spot that the state umbrella was no more than a golf umbrella? What was there about that pest of a boy that always made him come to grief?

I'll never believe a word he says again, thought Mr Goon, picking up the telephone receiver. Never in this world! He's a snake in the grass! He's a – a toad-in-the-hole. No – that's a pudding. Talking about me working with him! What sauce! What cheek! What . . .

Letting your tongue go loose too, he went on thinking. What does he mean? Let's try it – abbledy, abbledy, abbledy . . .

'What's that you say?' asked a surprised voice at the other end, and Mr Goon jumped. 'Er – can I speak to Chief Inspector Jenks, please?' he asked.

The conversation between the Inspector and Mr Goon was short, and much more satisfactory to Mr Goon than he had dared to hope. Apparently Inspector Jenks *was* annoyed with Fatty, and although a little sarcastic about people who believed in false princesses and particularly in state umbrellas, he said far less than Mr Goon had feared.

'All right, Goon,' he finished. 'Now, for pity's sake, put your best foot forward, and get something sensible done. It's in your district. Go and interview the boys up in the camp, use your brains, and PRODUCE RESULTS!'

'Yes, sir,' said Goon. 'And about that boy, Frederick Trotteville, sir – he's not to . . .'

But the Chief Inspector had rung off, and Goon stared at the silent receiver crossly. He had meant to put in a few well-chosen remarks about Fatty's shocking deception, and now it was too late.

Fatty told the others the result of his telephone call to the Chief Inspector, and of his interview with Mr Goon. Bets was sorry for Mr Goon. She didn't like him any more than the others did, but all the same she thought he hadn't had quite a fair deal this time – and it was really her fault because she had passed herself off so gleefully as the Princess Bongawee!

'We really will try to help him this time,' she said. 'We'll pass him on anything we find out.'

'He probably won't believe a word,' said Fatty. 'Still, we could pass anything on through Ern. He might believe Ern.'

Ern was still there. He looked alarmed. 'Here, don't you go telling me things to pass on to my uncle,' he protested. 'I don't want nothing to do with him. He don't like me, and I don't like him.'

'Well, Ern, it would only be to help him,' said Bets, earnestly. 'I feel rather awful about everything really – especially about the bit where I called him "frog face" in broken English!'

Fatty laughed. 'Gosh, I'd forgotten about that. Fancy *you* doing that, young Bets! He'll be calling you a toad, if you call him a frog!'

'It was awfully rude of me,' said Bets. 'I can't think what came over me. Ern, you *will* pass on anything we want you to, to your uncle, won't you?'

Ern couldn't resist Bets. He had a tremendous

admiration for her. He rubbed his hand over his untidy hair, and stared helplessly at her.

'All right,' he said. 'I'll do what you say. But mind, I don't promise he'll believe me. And I'm not going too near him either. I'll tell him over a fence or something. You don't know what a temper my uncle's got.'

'Oh yes, we do,' said Fatty, remembering some very nasty spurts of temper that Mr Goon had shown in the past. 'We don't *really* want to help him, Ern, but we do want to make up for messing him about this time, that's all. We'll make amends, if we can't be friends.'

'I say! That last bit sounds like portry,' said Ern.

> We'll make amends,
> If we can't be friends.

'See? It's portry, isn't it?'

'No, it just happened to rhyme, that's all,' said Fatty. 'By the way, you used to write a lot of poetry, er, portry, I mean. Ern, do you still write it?'

'Not so much,' said Ern, regretfully. 'It don't seem to come, like. I keep on starting pomes, but that's as far as I get. You know, just the first line or two, that's all. But I've got one here that's three lines almost.'

'Oh Ern, read it!' said Daisy, delighted. Ern's poems were always so very dismal and gloomy, and he was so very serious over them.

Ern fumbled in his pocket and brought out a dirty little notebook with a pencil hanging to it by a string. He licked his thumb and began to turn the pages.

'Here we are,' he said, and cleared his throat solemnly. He struck an attitude, and began to recite his 'pome' haltingly.

A pore old gardener said, "Ah me!
My days is almost done,
I've got rheumatics . . ."

Ern stopped and looked at the others in despair. 'I got stuck there,' he said. 'That's what always happens to me. I just get stuck – in the very middle of a good pome too. Took me two hours and twenty-one minutes to get that far. I timed meself. And now I can't finish it.'

'Yes, I can tell it would be a good pome,' said Fatty, solemnly. 'It goes like this, Ern.'

And Fatty also struck an attitude, legs apart, hands behind his back, face turned upwards – and recited glibly, without stopping.

A pore old gardener said, "Ah me!
My days is almost done,
I've got rheumatics in my knee,
And now it's hard to run.
I've got a measle in my foot,
And chilblains on my nose,
And bless me if I haven't got
Pneumonia in my toes.
All my hair has fallen out,
My teeth have fallen in,
I'm really getting rather stout,
Although I'm much too thin.
My nose is deaf, my ears are dumb,
My tongue is tied in knots,
And now my barrow and my spade
Have all come out in spots.
My watering can is . . ."

Larry shouted with laughter and Pip thumped Fatty on the back, yelling. Bets collapsed with Daisy on the rug. 'Don't,' said Bets. 'Stop, Fatty! How do you do it!'

Fatty stopped, out of breath. 'Had enough?' he said. 'I was just coming to where the watering can was feeling washed out, and the spade was feeling on edge, and . . .'

'*Don't*, Fatty!' begged Bets again, giggling helplessly. 'Oh dear – HOW do you do it?'

Only Ern was silent, without a smile or a laugh. He sat on the edge of a chair, struck with absolute wonder. He gazed at Fatty, and swallowed hard. He couldn't make it out. How could Fatty stand there and recite all that without thinking about it?

'Struck dumb, all of a sudden?' asked Fatty, amused. 'How do you like the way your "pome" goes on, Ern? It's a pity you didn't finish it, you know. You could have read it out to us then, instead of my saying it to you.'

Ern was even more bewildered. He blinked at Fatty. 'Do you mean to say, if I had finished that pome that's what it would have been like?' he asked, in an awed voice.

'Well, it's your pome, isn't it?' said Fatty cheerfully. 'I mean, I only just went on with it. I think you work too hard at your pomes, Ern. You just want to throw them off, so to speak. Like this.'

> The little Princess Bongawee
> Was very small and sweet,
> A princess from her pretty head
> Down to her tiny feet.
> She had a servant, Ern by name,
> A very stout young fella,
> Who simply loved to shield her with
> A dazzling . . .

'STATE UMBRELLA!' yelled everyone, except Ern. There were more yells and laughs. Ern didn't join in. He simply couldn't understand how Fatty could be so clever. Fatty gave him a thump.

'Ern! Wake up! You look daft, sitting there without a smile on your face. What's up?'

'You're a genius, Fatty, that's what's up,' said Ern. 'The others don't know it, because they don't know how difficult it is to write portry. But I do. And you stand there and – and . . .'

'Spout it out,' said Fatty. 'It's easy, that kind of stuff. I'm not a genius, Ern. Anyone can do that kind of thing, if they think about it.'

'But that's just it,' said Ern. 'You don't even think about it. It's like turning on a tap. Out it comes. Coo, lovaduck! If I could do portry like that, I'd think meself cleverer than the King of England.'

'Then you'd be wrong,' said Fatty. 'Cheer up, Ern. One of these days, your portry will come gushing out and then you'll be miserable because you won't be able to write it down fast enough.'

'I'd get a shock if it did,' said Ern, putting away his dirty little notebook with a sigh. 'I'm proud to know you, Fatty. If the others don't know a genius when they see one, I do. I'm not a very clever fellow, but I know good brains when I come across them. I tell you, you're a genius.'

This was a very remarkable speech indeed from Ern. The others looked at him in surprise. Was there more in Ern than they suspected? Bets slipped her hand through Fatty's arm.

'You're right, Ern,' she said. '*I* think Fatty's a genius too. But not only in poetry. In everything!'

Fatty looked pleased but extremely embarrassed.

He squeezed Bets' hand. He coughed modestly, and then coughed again, trying to think of something to say. But Larry spoke first, amused at Fatty's modest coughs.

> It was a coff,
> That carried him off,
> It was a coffin
> They carried him offin,

he said in a solemn and lugubrious voice. Whereupon the meeting dissolved in squeals of laughter and yells and thumps. Ern was delighted. What a set of WONDERFUL friends he had!

10. UP AT THE CAMP

That afternoon, Fatty began to 'investigate' in earnest. He had studied the papers, but had learnt very little from them. Apparently, the little prince had joined in a camp singsong the night he had disappeared, and had then had some cocoa and gone off to his tent with the three other boys he shared it with.

These three boys could give no help at all. They had been tired and had fallen asleep immediately they had got into their sleeping-bags. When they awoke, it was morning, and the prince's sleeping-bag was empty.

That was all they could say.

There's not very much to go on, thought Fatty. I suppose someone has kidnapped the boy. I'll have to question Ern and Sid and Perce, though I don't expect any of them know a thing – and I'll have to snoop round the camp a bit too, and keep my ears open.

He cycled round to Pip's that afternoon and found Larry and Daisy there. 'Has anyone got a relation of some sort up at the camping ground?' asked Fatty. 'I haven't as many relations as you have. Larry, can't you produce a cousin or something who might be staying at the camp?'

'No,' said Larry. 'What about you, Pip?'

'What schools are up there?' said Pip. 'Where's the paper? I saw a list of them today.'

They scanned the list carefully. 'Ah, there are boys from Lillington-Peterhouse,' said Pip. 'I know a cousin of mine goes there. He might be at the camp.'

'What's his name?' asked Fatty.

'Ronald Hilton,' said Pip. 'He's older than I am.'

'We could go and find the Lillington-Peterhouse lot,' said Fatty, 'and ask for Ronald. If he's there, you can have a powwow and the rest of us will have a snoop round, and keep our ears open.'

'I don't much want to have a powwow with Ronald,' said Pip. 'He'll think it awful cheek. I tell you, he's older than I am.'

'Do you realise this may be a mystery?' said Fatty severely. 'I know it doesn't seem like one at all, and we've begun all wrong, somehow – but it's a *possible* mystery, so it's your duty to do what you can, Pip.'

'Right,' said Pip, meekly. 'I'll powwow then. But if I get a clip on the ear, come and rescue me. I hope if it's a mystery, it livens up a bit. I can't get up much interest in a little foreign prince being kidnapped.'

'Nor can I,' admitted Daisy. 'But you never know. I bet we don't get much out of Ern, Sid, or Perce, Fatty. They wouldn't notice anything if it went on under their noses!'

'Got your bikes, Larry and Daisy?' asked Fatty. 'Come on then, let's go. We won't use the ferry, we'll go round by the bridge and up to the camp that way. It's not very far on bikes.'

They set off, with Buster as usual in Fatty's basket. He sat up there, perky and proud, looking down his nose at any other dog he met.

'If you get any bigger I won't be able to take you in my basket much longer, Buster,' panted Fatty, as he toiled up a hill.

'Woof,' agreed Buster, politely. He turned round and tried to lick Fatty's nose, but Fatty dodged.

They got to the camp at last. It was in a very

large field, sloping down to the river on one side. Clumps of trees stood here and there. Tents were everywhere, and smoke rose from where a meal was cooking. Boys hurried about, yelling and laughing.

The Find-Outers put their bicycles against a hedge. Fatty spoke to a boy coming along.

'Hey! Where's the Lillington-Peterhouse lot?'

The boy jerked his head towards the river. 'Last tents down there.'

The five children strolled down to the tents. Pip looked nervous. He really didn't like accosting a cousin two years older than himself, and very much bigger. He hoped he wouldn't see him.

But in a moment or two, he got a thump on the back and a cheerful-faced boy, three inches taller than Pip, shouted at him.

'Philip! What are *you* doing? Don't say you've come to look me up!'

Pip turned round. He grinned. 'Hello Ronald!' he said. 'Yes, I did come to look you up. Hope you don't mind.'

It was funny to hear Pip being called by his right name, Philip. Pip introduced his cousin to the others. Ronald stared hard at Fatty.

'Hey! Aren't you the chap Philip is always gassing about – the one that works with the police or something?'

Fatty looked modest. 'Well, I do help the police sometimes,' he admitted.

'Are you on a job now?' asked Ronald eagerly. 'Come and tell us about it!'

'No – no, I can't,' said Fatty. 'We've just come up here to see you – and out of interest because of the disappearance of that young prince.'

'Oh, that fellow!' said Ronald, leading them all into a very spacious tent. 'Don't bother about *him*! Jolly good riddance, *I* say! He was the most awful little beast imaginable!'

There was a long wooden table in the tent and on it were spread plates of jam sandwiches, potted meat sandwiches, buns, and slices of fruit cake. Jugs of lemonade stood at intervals down the length of the table.

'You do well for yourselves!' said Larry.

'Help yourselves,' invited Ronald. 'I'm helping with the catering this week – head cook and bottlewasher, you know. It's a bit early for tea, but everything's ready and we might as well get what we want before the hungry hordes rush in.'

They each got plates, and piled them with food. It really was not more than an hour or so since they had finished their lunches, but that made no difference. All of them could eat, hungrily, at any time of the day or night, including Buster, who was now sniffing about under the table, snapping up all kinds of tasty bits and pieces.

Ronald led them out into the field again, complete with plates of food, and took them down to the river. 'Come on, we'll sit and eat in peace here,' he said. 'My word, Trotteville, I'm pleased to meet you. Philip's told me no end of tales about you at one time and another – and I've told them to my pals too.'

Fatty told him a few more, and enjoyed himself very much. Pip got bored. His cousin took no further notice of him, he was so wrapped up in Fatty. Pip finished his tea and got up. He beckoned to Larry.

'Come on, let's go for a wander round,' he said. 'We might pick up something.'

They strolled round the field. Nobody took much notice of them. Larry stopped a boy going by. 'Where's the tent Prince Bongawah slept in?' he asked.

'Over there, if it's any interest to you!' said the boy cheekily, and hurried off.

Pip and Larry walked over to the tent he had pointed out. Outside sat three boys, munching sandwiches. They were all about Pip's age.

'Good tent, yours,' said Larry to the boys. It certainly was a very fine one indeed, much better than any other tent nearby.

'Supplied by his Royal Highness, Prince Bongawah-wah-wah,' said one of the boys.

Pip laughed. 'Why do you call him that?' he asked. 'Didn't you like him?'

'No,' said the boys, all together. A red-haired one waved his sandwich at Larry.

'He was a frightful, cocky little fellow,' he said. 'And a real idiot. He yelled at everything, like a kid of seven!'

'That's why we called him Wah-wah,' said another boy. 'He was always wah-wahing about something.'

'Did he talk English?' asked Larry.

'Well, he was supposed to know hardly a word,' said Red-Hair. 'He just talked rubbish usually – but he could speak our language all right if he wanted to! Though goodness knows where he picked it up! Talk about Cockney!'

'What school did he go to?' asked Larry.

'None. He had a tutor,' said Red-Hair. 'He was a regular little urchin, for all he was a prince! All his clothes were of the very very best, even his pyjamas – but did he wash? Not he! And if you said you'd pop him into the river he'd run a mile, wah-wahing!'

'Lots of boys are like that,' said the third boy, munching away. 'We've got two at our school. One never cleans his teeth and the other howls if he gets a kick at football.'

'Do you think the prince got kidnapped?' asked Pip, feeling rather thrilled with all this first-hand information.

'I don't know and I don't care,' said Red-Hair. 'If he *is* kidnapped, I hope he stays kidnapped, that's all. Have a look at his sleeping-bag. Did you ever see one like it?'

Larry and Pip peeped inside the marvellous tent. Red-Hair pointed to a sleeping-bag at one side. It certainly was most magnificent, padded and quilted and marvelously embroidered.

'Try it,' said Red-Hair. 'I tried it once. It's like being floated away on a magic carpet or something when you get inside – soft as feathers!'

Pip wriggled inside. It certainly was an extraordinarily luxurious bag, and Pip felt that if he closed his eyes he would be wafted away into sleep at once. He wriggled down a little further and felt something hard against his leg. He put his hand down to feel what it was.

It was a button! A very fine button too, blue with a gold edge. Pip sat up and looked at it. Red-Hair glanced at it.

'One of the buttons off his pyjamas,' he said. 'You should have seen them! Blue and gold with those buttons to match.'

'Do you think I might keep it as a souvenir?' said Pip. He really wondered if by any chance it might turn out to be a clue!

'Gosh, what do you want a souvenir for? Are you daft?' said the second boy. 'Keep it if you want to. I don't reckon Wah-wah will want it again! If he loses a button, he'll be provided with a new set of pyjamas!'

'Did he leave his pyjamas behind?' asked Larry, thinking it might be a good idea to look at them.

'No. He went off in them,' said Red-Hair. 'That's what makes everyone think he was kidnapped. He'd have dressed himself if he had run away.'

Larry and Pip wandered out into the open air again. A loud voice suddenly hailed them.

'Larry! Pip! What you doing up here?' And there was Ern's plump face grinning at them from over the nearby hedge. 'Come on over! We've got *our* tent here!'

11. A LITTLE INVESTIGATION

'Hello, Ern!' said Larry, surprised. He had forgotten that Ern had been camping so near the big camp field. The faces of Sid and Perce now appeared, Perce grinning, Sid very solemn as usual.

Larry and Pip said good-bye to Red-Hair and his friends and squeezed through the hedge to Ern. Pip had put the pyjama button safely into his pocket. He didn't know whether it might be useful or not.

Ern proudly showed the two boys his tent. It was a very small and humble affair, compared with the magnificent one they had just left – but Ern, Sid, and Perce were intensely proud of it. They had never been camping before, and were enjoying it immensely.

There were no sleeping bags in the tent, merely old, worn rugs spread over a groundsheet. Three mugs, three broken knives, three spoons, two forks ('Perce lost his when he was bathing,' was Ern's mystifying explanation), three macintosh capes, three enamel plates, and a few other things.

'Fine, isn't it?' said Ern. 'We get water from the tap over in the camp field. They let us use it if we just go straight there and back. But they won't let the caravanners use it. So we get it for them, and in return they sometimes cook us a meal.'

There were a good many caravans scattered about, and also one or two more small tents. The caravan standing next to Ern's tent was empty, and a litter of papers was blowing about.

'The people there have gone,' said Ern. 'There was a woman and two kids – the kids were babies. Twins like Perce and Sid.'

'Ar,' said Sid, who was following them about, chewing. 'Ar.'

'What's he mean, arr-ing like that?' asked Pip, annoyed. 'Can't he ever talk properly?'

'Not while he has toffee in his mouth,' said Ern. 'Ma don't allow him so much when he's at home, of course, so he talks a bit more there. But here, when he can eat toffee all day long, he never says much except "Ar". Do you, young Sid?'

'Ar,' said Sid, trying to swallow the rest of

his toffee quickly, and almost choking.

'He seems to want to say something,' said Pip, interestedly. 'Do you, Sid?'

'Ar,' said Sid frantically, going purple in the face.

'Oh, it's only to tell you about the twin babies, I expect,' said Ern. 'He was cracked on them, was our Sid. He used to go over to that caravan and pore over the pram for hours on end. He's dippy on babies.'

Pip and Larry looked at Sid with surprise. He didn't seem at all the kind of boy to be 'dippy on babies'.

Sid pointed down to the ground, where there were four different sets of pram wheel marks.

'There you are, you see – I said he wanted to tell you about them twins,' said Ern. 'He used to stand by their pram and pick up all the rattles and things they dropped. I bet he's ready to howl now they're gone. He's a funny one, Sid is.'

'Ar,' said Sid, in a strangled voice, and almost choked again.

'You're disgusting,' said Ern. 'You and your toffee. You've et a whole tin since yesterday. I'll tell Ma on you. You go and spit it out.'

Sid wandered away, evidently giving up all hope of proper conversation. Pip heaved a sigh of relief. Sid and his toffee gave him a nightmare feeling.

'Sid was proper upset this morning, when the twins went,' said Perce, entering amicably into the conversation. 'He went over to joggle the pram like he does when their mother wants them to go to sleep – but she yelled at him and chased him away. That made the babies yell too, and there wasn't half a set-to.'

'What did she want to do that to our Sid for?' said Ern, quite annoyed at anyone yelling at his Sid. 'He's been good to those smelly kids, he's wheeled their big pram up and down the field for hours.'

Pip and Larry were getting tired of all this talk about Sid and the babies. Who cared anyway?

'Ern, did you hear anything at all last night when Prince Bongawah was supposed to be kidnapped?' asked Larry. 'Did Sid or Perce?'

'No. We none of us heard anything,' said Ern, firmly. 'We all sleep like tops. Sid don't even wake if there is a thunderstorm bang over his head. The whole camp could have been kidnapped, and we wouldn't have known a thing. Good sleepers, the Goons are.'

Well, that was that. There didn't seem to be anything at all to be got from Ern. How maddening to know someone living just across the hedge from the prince, and to get nothing out of him at all!

'You did *see* the prince though, didn't you?' said Larry.

'Yes. I told you,' said Ern. 'He was a funny little fellow with a cocky little face. He made faces.'

'Made faces?' said Larry, in astonishment. 'What do you mean?'

'Well, whenever Sid or Perce or me peeped through the hedge, he'd see us and make a face,' said Ern. 'He may have been a prince, but he hadn't been brought up proper. Brown as a berry, of course.'

'Browner than us?' asked Pip.

''Bout the same,' said Ern.

'Why did you say that he and Bets were as alike as peas in a pod?' asked Pip, suddenly remembering this extraordinary remark of Ern's.

Ern blushed. 'Oh well, seemed as if brother and sister ought to look alike,' he muttered, and busily kicked a stone along. 'Coo, I wonder what happened to his state umbrella! You should have seen it, Pip. Somebody came to visit him, and one of them put up this enormous umbrella – all blue and gold it was – and carried it over him. He didn't half scowl.'

'Didn't he like it then?' asked Pip.

'Well, everyone laughed and yelled and shouted,' said Ern. 'It looked a bit strange, you know.'

'Hello there!' suddenly came Fatty's voice over the hedge. 'Why did you wander off like that? You left me to do all the talking, Pip.'

'That's why I went,' said Pip. 'You like talking, Fatty, don't you?'

'Can we come through the hedge?' called Daisy's voice. 'Is there a place where we won't tear our clothes?'

Ern gallantly held aside some prickly branches as the girls squeezed through the hedge. Fatty followed. 'Nice cousin of yours, that fellow Ronald,' Fatty said to Pip. 'We had quite a chat.'

'You must have done quite a lot of "questioning of witnesses" then,' said Pip slyly, remembering the books Fatty had been studying a day or two before.

'Did you get any interesting information about this case?'

'Well, no,' said Fatty, who had actually spent the whole time relating some of his own exploits to the open-mouthed Ronald. 'No. I didn't gather much.'

'What about you, Pip?' asked Bets. 'Have you been questioning Ern, Sid and Perce?'

'Yes,' said Pip. 'But Larry and I didn't get much out of them. They slept all night long and didn't hear a thing. They haven't the faintest idea what happened to Prince Bongawah.'

'Ar,' said Sid, joining them suddenly. His jaws chewed frantically. Pip looked at him in disgust.

'Go away,' he said. 'And don't come back till you can say something else. I shall start "arring" myself in a minute. ARRRRRRRR!'

He made such a fierce noise that Sid gave him an alarmed glance and fled.

Pip took out the blue and gold button from his pocket and showed it to the others.

'This is the solitary clue – if it can be called a clue – that we've found,' he said. 'I found it in the sleeping bag belonging to the prince. It came off his blue and gold pyjamas.'

'Well, what use do you think that is?' asked Fatty. 'Is it going to help us to find out who kidnapped the prince, or when or how, or where he's gone? Not much of a clue, Pip.'

'No,' said Pip, pocketing the button again. 'I thought it wasn't. But you always tell us to examine everything and keep everything just in case. So I did. By the way, he didn't dress, he disappeared in his pyjamas.'

That made Fatty stare. 'Are you sure, Pip? Who told you?'

'The boys who slept in his tent,' said Pip.

'Well, that's funny,' said Fatty.

'Why?' asked Daisy. 'There wouldn't be any time, would there, for him to dress? Besides, wouldn't he disturb the other boys if he did?'

'Not if he stole outside in the dark when they were asleep,' said Fatty. 'He could take his clothes with him and dress quickly. Anyone wandering about in pyjamas would be spotted.'

'But Fatty, surely there wouldn't be *time* for anyone to dress if he was being kidnapped,' said Daisy again. 'They'd just grab the prince out of his tent and make off with him, in his pyjamas.'

'Oh no, Daisy,' said Fatty. 'You're not being very clever. Kidnappers would never creep through a crowded field, falling over tent ropes and pegs, finding their way to one special tent, opening the flap, dragging out one special boy in the darkness, who would surely yell the place down. After all, he was called Bongawah-wah-wah because he howled so much.'

'Oh,' said Daisy. 'Yes, that was very silly of me. Of course kidnappers wouldn't do it like that. What do you think they did?'

'I think somebody arranged for him to steal out after lights-out,' said Fatty. 'Perhaps they said they'd take him to that Fair in the next town – it goes on till all hours! Something like that. You can't tell. And if he was going to be kidnapped, the kidnappers would find it easy – there he would be, waiting at the gate for them, already dressed, thinking what a lad he was.'

'I see – and they'd just whisk him away in a car and that would be that,' said Pip.

'Oh, *now* I see why you're surprised he was in pyjamas,' said Daisy. 'If the kidnapping was planned in that way, he certainly wouldn't be in pyjamas!'

'Correct,' said Fatty, with a grin.

'Maybe he couldn't spot his clothes in the darkness,' suggested Ern, helpfully.

'This isn't a mystery, it's a silly sort of puzzle,' said Bets. 'Nobody heard anything, nobody saw anything. Nobody knows anything. I'm beginning to feel it couldn't have happened!'

12. SID FINDS HIS VOICE

'Come on – it's time we went,' said Fatty, getting bored. 'We're absolutely at a dead end here. Wherever Prince Bongawah is, he's probably still in his blue and gold pyjamas. Good luck to him!'

They rode off, waving good-bye to Ern and Perce. Sid was nowhere to be seen, for which everyone was thankful.

'He chews his toffee like a cow chewing the cud,' said Pip. 'Have you noticed how spotty he is? I really do believe he lives on toffee and nothing else.'

'I never want to see him again,' said Bets. 'He makes me feel sick.'

'Well, there's no reason why we ever *should* see him again,' said Fatty. 'So long as Ern comes alone to see us. *I* don't intend to visit dear Sid and Perce.'

But he did see Sid again, and that very evening too! Fatty was trying on one of his newest disguises down in his shed, when there came a knock at the door.

Fatty looked through a hole, pierced in the door for spying, to see who was outside. Gosh – it was Ern – with Sid! How aggravating, just as he was going to practise this disguise.

Fatty turned quickly and looked at himself in the big mirror. He grinned. He'd try the disguise out on Ern and see if it worked!

Fatty opened the door. Ern stood outside, ready with a smile. Sid beside him. The smile faded as Ern saw, not Fatty, but a bent old man with side-whiskers, a straggly beard, shaggy white eyebrows, and wispy white hair on a bald pate. He was dressed in a loose, ill-fitting old coat, with dragged-down pockets, and corduroy trousers, wrinkled and worn.

'Oh, er, good evening,' said Ern, startled. 'Is, er, is Mr Frederick Trotteville in?'

The old man put a trembling hand behind one ear and said, 'Speak up! Don't mumble. What's that you say?' His voice was as quavery as his hand.

Ern shouted, 'IS MR FREDERICK IN?'

'Now don't you shout,' said the old man, in a

cross voice. 'I'm not deaf. Who's Mr Frederick?'

Ern stared. Then he remembered that Fatty was always called Fatty. Perhaps this old man only knew him by that name.

'Fatty,' he said, loudly. 'FATTY.'

'You're a very rude boy,' said the old man, his voice quavering higher. 'Calling me names.'

'I'm not,' said Ern, desperately. 'Look here – where's the boy who lives here?'

'Gone,' said the old fellow, shaking his head, sadly. 'Gone to live in London.'

Ern began to think he must be in a dream. Fatty gone to London! Why, he'd only seen him an hour or so ago. He glanced anxiously at the shed. Had he come to the right place?

'Why has he gone?' he asked at last. 'Did he leave a message? And what are you doing here?'

'I'm his caretaker,' said the old fellow, and took out a big red handkerchief. He proceeded to blow his nose with such a loud trumpeting noise that Ern fell back, alarmed. Little did he know that Fatty was hiding his gulps of laughter in that big red handkerchief!

Sid backed away too. He slid down the path

but Ern caught him by the arm.

'Oh no, you don't, Sid! You've come here to say something important, and say it you're going to, if it takes us all night to find Fatty. If you go back to the camp, you'll fill your mouth with toffee again, and we won't none of us get a word out of you! You're the only one of us with a real clue, and Fatty's going to know it!'

'I *say*! Has he really got a clue?' said the old man, in Fatty's crisp, clear voice. Ern jumped violently and looked all round. Where was Fatty?

The old man dug him in the ribs and went off into a cackle of laughter that changed suddenly into Fatty's cheerful guffaw. Ern stared at him open-mouthed. So did Sid.

'Lovaduck! It's *Fatty*!' cried Ern, overjoyed and astounded. 'You took me in properly. Coo, you're an old man to the life. How do you make yourself bald?'

'Just a wig,' said Fatty, lifting it off his head and appearing in his own thatch of hair. He grinned. 'I was practising this disguise when you came. It's a new wig, and new eyebrows, side-whiskers, and beard to match. Good, aren't they?'

'You're a marvel, Fatty, honest you are,' said

Ern, wonderstruck. 'But your voice – and your laugh! You can't buy *them*! You ought to be on the stage.'

'Can't,' said Fatty. 'I'm going to be a detective. It's a help to be a good actor, of course. Come in. What's all this about Sid and a clue?'

'Well,' said Ern solemnly, 'it's like this. Sid wanted to tell us all something this afternoon and he couldn't, because of his toffee. Well, he worked and he worked at his toffee till it all went.'

'Tiring work,' said Fatty, sympathetically. 'And then, I suppose, he found his voice again. Can he really say something besides "ar"?'

'Well, not much,' said Ern honestly. 'But he did tell us something very strange – very strange indeed, Fatty. So I've brought him down here to tell *you*. It may be very, very important. Go on, Sid – you tell him.'

Sid cleared his throat and opened his mouth. 'Ar,' he began. 'Ar – you see, I heard them yelling. Ar, I did.'

'Who was yelling?' enquired Fatty.

'Ar, well,' said Sid, and cleared his throat again. 'They were yelling, see.'

'Yes. We know that,' said Fatty. 'Ar.'

That put Sid off. He gazed beseechingly at Ern. Ern looked back forbiddingly.

'See what happens to you when you get toffee mad?' he said. 'You lose your voice and you lose your senses. Let this be a lesson to you, young Sid.'

'Has he really come just to tell me somebody was yelling?' asked Fatty. 'Isn't there anything else?'

'Oh, yes. But praps *I'd* better tell you,' said Ern, and Sid's face cleared at once.

'Ar,' he said.

'And don't you interrupt,' said Ern, threateningly. Sid had no intention of interrupting at all. He shook his head vigorously, not even venturing another 'ar'.

'Well, this is what Sid told us,' said Ern, beginning to enjoy himself. 'It's peculiar, Fatty, honest it is. You'll hardly believe it.'

'Oh, get *on* Ern,' said Fatty. 'This may be important. Begin at the beginning, please.'

'I told you – at least I told Larry and Pip – that our Sid here is mad on babies,' said Ern. 'He's always going about joggling their prams and picking up their toys and saying "Goo" to them.

Well, next to our tent there's a caravan – you saw it. It's empty now. The people went today.'

Fatty nodded. He was listening hard.

'The woman in the caravan had a couple of twin babies,' said Ern. 'And being twins, Sid got more interested in them than usual – him and Perce being twins, you see. So he played with them a lot. Didn't you, Sid?'

'Ar,' said Sid, nodding.

'Well, this morning, Sid heard those babies yelling like anything,' said Ern, warming up to his tale. 'And he went over to joggle the pram. The woman was in the caravan, packing up, and when she saw our Sid there, she flew out at him and smacked him on the head. A fair clip it was! She told him to clear off.'

'Why?' asked Fatty. 'Sid was only doing what he'd been in the habit of doing. Had the woman ever objected before?'

'No,' said Ern. 'She let him wheel them up and sometimes down, too. And a heavy job it was, because it's a big double pram, made to take twins. Well, she smacked his head and Sid went off, upset like.'

'I don't wonder,' said Fatty, wondering when the point of all this long tale was coming. 'What came next?'

'The woman dragged the pram round to the back of the caravan,' said Ern, 'where she could keep her eye on it. But those babies still went on yelling, and our Sid here, he couldn't bear it.'

'Ar,' said Sid, feelingly.

'So when the woman took some things and went off down to one of the other caravans, Sid popped over to the pram to see what was the matter with the babies,' said Ern. 'They sounded as if they was sitting on a safety pin or something. Anyway, Sid put his hand down under them and scrabbled about like – *and he felt somebody else down in that big pram*, Fatty!'

Fatty was really startled. He sat up straight. 'Somebody else!' he said, incredulously. 'What do you mean?'

'Well – just that,' said Ern. 'Sid felt somebody else, and he pulled the clothes back just a little bit, and saw the back of a dark head, and a bit of dark cheek. Then one of the babies grabbed at Sid, and rolled over and hid whoever it was in the pram.'

Fatty was astounded. He sat silent for a minute. Then he looked at Sid. 'Who did you think it was in the pram?' he asked.

'The prince,' said Sid, quite forgetting to say 'ar' in his excitement. 'He was hiding there. He didn't know I saw him. Ar.'

'*Well*!' said Fatty, taking all this in. 'So *that's* what happened. He simply crept out of his tent in his pyjamas, and hid in the caravan for the night – and in the early morning, the woman packed him into the bottom of that big pram, hidden under the babies! How uncomfortable! He must have been all screwed up – and awfully hot.'

'Ar,' said Sid, nodding.

'Then the woman must have got someone to fetch all her goods, and wheeled the pram away herself, with the little prince in it,' said Fatty. 'Nobody would guess. But why did it happen? What has *she* got to do with it? Why did the prince creep away to her? Gosh – it's a mystery all right!'

'I thought you'd be pleased, Fatty,' said Ern, happily. 'Good thing Sid got rid of his toffee, wasn't it? That's what he was trying to tell us this afternoon. Almost choked himself trying to get the news out.'

'It's a pity he didn't tell somebody as soon as he knew this,' said Fatty.

'He did try,' said Ern. 'But I just thought he wanted to go swimming or something when he kept pointing to the caravan. Sid's never very talkative, even in the ordinary way. His tongue never grew properly, Ma says.'

'I'll have to think what to do,' said Fatty. 'Ern, you must go and tell your uncle. I said we'd tell him everything we found out. You'd better go and tell him straight away.'

'Lovaduck! I can't do that!' said poor Ern. 'Why, he'd give me such a scolding that I wouldn't recover for a month of Sundays!'

13. MR. GOON HEARS THE NEWS

All the same, Ern had to go. Fatty didn't want to ring up the Chief Inspector quite so soon after his ticking-off – and if Goon knew, he could report the matter himself. So poor Ern was sent off to Goon's with Sid trailing behind. Neither of them felt very happy about it.

Mr Goon was in his kitchen at the back of his house. He was alone – and he was practising. Not disguises, like Fatty. He was trying to 'let his tongue go loose', as Fatty had advised. *Could* he 'talk foreign' by merely letting his tongue go loose?

He stood there, trying to make his tongue work. 'Abbledy, abbledy, abbledy,' he gabbled, and then paused. For some reason, 'abbledy' seemed the only thing he could think of. He tried to remember the string of foreign-sounding words that Fatty had fired off the other afternoon, but he couldn't. Surely it must be easy to say a string of rubbish?

But it wasn't. His tongue merely stopped when it was tired of saying 'abbledy', and his brain could think of nothing else at all.

Mr Goon tried reciting.

'The boy stood on the burning deck, abbledy, gabbledy, abbledy. No, it's no good.'

Meanwhile, Ern and Sid had arrived. Ern didn't like to knock in case his uncle was having a nap, as he so often did. He turned the handle of the front door. It wouldn't open, so he thought it must be locked from the inside.

'Come on round to the back, Sid,' said Ern. 'He might be in the garden.'

They tiptoed round to the back, and came to the kitchen window. It was wide open. A noise came from inside the room. 'He's there,' whispered Ern. 'He's talking. He must have a visitor.'

They listened. 'Abbledy, abbledy, abbledy,' they heard. 'Abbledy, abbledy, ABBLEDY.'

Ern looked at Sid, startled. That was his uncle's voice. What was he gabbling about? Ern cautiously poked his head a bit further forward and peeped in at the corner of the window. Yes – his uncle was there with his back to him, standing on the rug, looking at himself in the mirror and gabbling his curious rubbish on and on.

Ern didn't like it at all. Had his uncle got a stroke of the sun? Was he out of his mind?

'Abbledy, abbledy,' came again and again. And then, suddenly, 'The boy stood on the burning deck.'

That decided Ern. He wasn't going to interfere in anything like this, important clue or not. He stole down by the side of the house, and made his way to the front gate. But alas, Mr Goon had heard footsteps, and was at the front door at once. He was just in time to see Ern and Sid opening the gate.

'What you doing here this time of the evening?' he roared. 'What you doing going out before you've even come in? You been listening outside the window?'

Ern was terrified. He stood trembling at the gate with Sid.

'Uncle, we only came to tell you something,' quavered Ern. 'A clue. Most important.'

'Aha!' said Goon. 'So that's it. Come along in then. Why didn't you say so before?'

He just stopped himself saying, 'abbledy,

abbledy.' He must be careful. He'd gone and got that on his mind now!

Ern and Sid came in, treading like cats on hot bricks. Mr Goon took them into his sitting-room. He sat down in his big armchair, crossed his legs, put his hands together and looked up at the two boys.

'So you've got a clue,' he said. 'What is it?'

Sid couldn't say a word, of course, not even 'ar'. Ern was almost as bad. However, it all came out with a rush at last.

'Uncle, Sid found the clue. You know that Prince Bongawah that was kidnapped? Well, he wasn't. He put himself in a pram with twin babies and he was wheeled away this morning.'

Mr Goon listened to this with the utmost disbelief. Put himself in a pram? With twins! And got himself wheeled away! What nonsense was this?

Mr Goon rose up, big and terrible. 'And why did you come and tell me this ridiculous nonsense?' he began. 'Why don't you go and tell it to that big boy? Let *him* believe you! I won't. Cock-and-bull story! Gah! How DARE you come and tell me such a tale?'

'Fatty told us to,' blurted out poor Ern, almost crying with fright. 'We told him and *he* believed us. He said we were to tell *you*, Uncle, really he did. To help you.'

Mr Goon swelled up till Ern and Sid thought he must be going to burst all the buttons off his already-tight tunic. He towered above them.

'You go and tell that toad of a boy that I'm not such an idiot as he thinks I am,' he bellowed. 'You tell him to take his tales of prams and twin babies to the Chief Inspector. Sending you here to fill me up with nonsense like that! I'm ashamed of you, Ern. For two pins, I'd give you a hiding. How DARE you!'

Ern and Sid fled. They fled down the hall passage, through the front door, and out of the gate without waiting for another word. Sid was crying. Ern was white. Why had Fatty sent him on such an errand? He, Ern, had known quite well that his uncle wouldn't believe him. And he hadn't.

'Come on back to the camp,' panted Ern. 'We'll be safe there. Run, Sid, run!'

Poor Ern didn't even think of going back to Fatty's to tell him what had happened. He and Sid fled for their lives, looking over their shoulders every now and again, fearful that Mr Goon might be after them.

Perce was thankful he hadn't gone with them when he heard their tale. He was just as much scared of his uncle as the others. Ern had often told him and Sid dreadful tales of the time when he had been to stay with Mr Goon – the punishments and shoutings-at that he had had.

'Still, it was worth it,' Ern would end cheerfully. 'I made friends with those five kids – specially with Fatty. He's a wonder, that boy!'

Meantime the 'wonder boy' was having a quiet little think to himself about Sid's surprising piece of news. It was all very, very extraordinary. Could Sid possibly be right? Could it really have been the young prince huddled down in that big double pram? Of course, such a trick *had* been played before, to get people away in secret.

Just have to take out the two seats, put the person in the well of the pram, and stick the babies on top of him, thought Fatty. Yes – it's easy enough. But why, why, why, did the prince creep through the hedge at night and get himself parked in the pram the following day?

It was a puzzle. Fatty thought he had better sleep on it, and then discuss it with the others in the morning. He wondered what Mr Goon had thought of Ern's appearance and news. Was he acting on it? Had he telephoned the Chief Inspector?

Fatty half-expected Mr Goon to telephone him for his opinion on Ern's news. But no, on second thoughts he wouldn't, decided Fatty. He would want to work out things on his own, so that he could say he had done everything himself.

Well, let him, thought Fatty. If he can unravel the puzzle more quickly than I can, good luck to him! I'm in a real muddle. Why – when – where – how – and, particularly, *why*, seem quite unanswerable!

Fatty telephoned Larry.

'Is that you, Larry? Meet in my shed tomorrow morning, half past nine, sharp. Most important and mysterious developments. Ern and Sid have just been down with amazing news.'

'Great!' came Larry's voice, tense with excitement. 'What is it? Tell me a bit, Fatty!'

'Can't say it over the phone,' said Fatty. 'Anyway, it's most important. Half past nine sharp.'

He rang off, leaving Larry in a state of such terrific excitement that he could hardly prevent himself from rushing down to Fatty's at once! Daisy and he spent the whole evening trying to think of what Fatty's mysterious news could be – without any success, of course.

Fatty telephoned Pip next. Mrs Hilton answered the phone. 'Pip's in the bath,' she said. 'Can I take a message?'

Fatty hesitated. Mrs Hilton was not at all encouraging where mysteries were concerned. In fact, she had several times said that Pip and Bets must keep out of them. Perhaps, on the whole, it would be best not to say much. Still, he could ask for Bets.

So Bets came to the telephone, in her dressing-gown, having a feeling that Fatty had some news.

'Hello Fatty,' came her voice. 'Anything up?'

'Yes,' said Fatty, in a solemn voice. 'Extraordinary news has just come through – from Ern and Sid. Can't tell you over the phone. Meet here at half past nine tomorrow morning, sharp.'

'*Fatty*!' squealed Bets, thrilled. 'You *must* tell me

something about it. Quick! Nobody's about, it's quite safe.'

'I can't possibly tell you over the phone,' said Fatty, enjoying all this importance. 'All I can say is that it's very important, and will need a lot of discussion and planning. The real mystery is about to begin, Bets!'

'Ooooh,' said Bets. 'All right – half past nine tomorrow. I'll go straight away and tell Pip.'

'Now don't you go shouting all this through the bathroom door,' said Fatty, in alarm.

'No, I suppose I'd better not,' said Bets. 'I'll wait till he comes out. But I'll jolly well go and hurry him though!'

Pip was so thrilled at this sudden and unexpected telephone call that he, like Larry, almost felt inclined to dress and shoot off to Fatty. But as his mother would certainly be most annoyed to find him dressing again and going out after a hot bath, he reluctantly decided he must wait.

Fatty sat in his bedroom and thought. He thought hard, turning over in his mind all the things he knew about the young prince. He got the encyclopaedia and looked up Tetarua. He found a store catalogue of his mother's which, most fortunately, pictured not only a single pram but a double one as well, with measurements.

Fatty decided it would be the easiest thing in the world to hide someone at the bottom of a double pram. Probably the most uncomfortable thing in the world too, he thought. I wonder what old Goon is making of all this!

Goon wasn't making anything of it at all. He just simply didn't believe a word, so he had nothing to puzzle over. 'Gah!' he said, and dismissed the matter completely!

14. TALKING AND PLANNING

Before half past nine had struck, the Five Find-Outers (and Dog) were all gathered together in Fatty's shed. Buster was very pleased to welcome them. He pranced round in delight, and finally got on to Bets' knee.

'Now Fatty – don't keep us waiting – tell us exactly what's happened,' said Larry, firmly. 'Don't go all mysterious and solemn. Just tell us!'

So Fatty told them. They listened in astonishment.

'Hidden in the *pram*!' said Larry. 'Then the prince must have known that woman very well. She must have been camping nearby for a reason.'

'Do you think she could have been the prince's nurse, and knew perhaps he wasn't happy at camp, and arranged to smuggle him away?' said Bets.

'Bright idea, Bets,' said Fatty, approvingly. 'I thought of that myself. But the twin babies are rather a difficulty there. I don't feel the prince would have a nurse with twin babies somehow.'

'She might have been an *old* nurse of his, and got married, and had twins,' said Bets, using her imagination.

'It's not much good having theories and ideas about all this until we get a few more actual details,' said Fatty. 'I mean, we must find out who the woman is, if the caravan belongs to her, if she came there when the prince arrived, if those babies are really hers, or borrowed so that she could take that big double pram for hiding purposes – oh, there are a whole lot of things to find out!'

'And are we to snoop round and find all these details?' asked Daisy. 'I rather like doing that.'

'There's a great deal to find out,' said Fatty. 'We'll have to get busy. Anyone seen the papers this morning?'

'I just glanced at them,' said Larry, 'but I was really too excited to read anything. Why?'

'Only because there's a bit more about the prince and his country in today,' said Fatty. He spread a newspaper on the floor and pointed to a column.

Everyone read it.

'Well, as you will see,' said Fatty, 'Tetarua isn't a very big country, but it's quite important from the point of view of the British, because there's a fine airfield there we want to use. So we've been quite friendly with them.'

'And they've sent their young prince here to be educated,' said Larry. 'But, according to the paper, there's a row on in Tetarua between the present king and his cousin, who says *he* ought to be king.'

'Yes. And the possibilities are that the cousin has sent someone over here to capture Prince Bongawah, so that, if he doesn't ever appear again, he, the cousin, will be king,' said Fatty. 'There are no brothers or sisters apparently.'

'An old, old plot,' said Larry. 'Do you suppose they will demand a ransom for the prince?'

'No,' said Fatty. 'I think they want to put him out of the way for good.'

There was a silence after this. Nobody liked to think of the young prince being 'put away for good'. Bets shivered.

Daisy rubbed her forehead, puzzled. 'And yet – though that's what the papers say – *we* know differently,' she said. '*We* know he wasn't kidnapped in the way they think, just swept out of his tent and rushed off in a car somewhere. *We* know that, of his own free will, apparently, he crept out of his tent in his pyjamas, went through the hedge to that caravan, and allowed himself to be hidden and wheeled away in that pram! That couldn't be called kidnapping.'

'No. It couldn't,' said Fatty. 'There's something strange about this. I believe Sid, you know. For one thing, he would never, ever have the imagination to make up all that.'

'Did you ring the Chief Inspector?' said Pip. 'What did he say?'

'Well, as a matter-of-fact, I didn't telephone him,' said Fatty. 'I don't feel he's very pleased with me at the moment – with any of us, as a matter-of-fact – so I sent Ern and Sid round to Mr Goon, to tell *him*. He would naturally ring up the Chief Inspector himself, and get his own orders.'

'But wouldn't the Chief Inspector ring *you*, when he got Mr Goon's message?' asked Pip.

'I rather thought he might,' said Fatty, who was feeling a little hurt because there had been no word at all from the Chief Inspector. 'I expect he's still peeved with me. Well, I won't bother him till I've got something first rate to tell him. Let Mr Goon get on with his own ideas about this – we'll get on with ours! At least I've passed on Sid's information to him.'

There was another silence. 'It's rather a peculiar mystery really,' said Bets at last. 'There doesn't actually seem anywhere to *begin*. What do we do first?'

'Well, as *I* see it, we had better follow up the definite clues we have,' said Fatty. 'We must first of all find out about that woman – who she is. Get her address. Interview her. Try and frighten something out of her. If she is hiding the prince, we must find out where. And why.'

'Yes,' said Larry. 'We must do all that. Hadn't we better begin before Mr Goon gets going? He'll probably be working along the same lines as us.'

'Yes. I suppose he will,' said Fatty, getting up. 'This part is pretty obvious to anyone – even to Mr Goon! Well, let's hope we don't bump into him today. He'll be annoyed if we do!'

'Woof,' said Buster joyfully.

'He says he hopes we *do* bump into him,' said

Bets, hugging the little Scottie. 'You love Mr Goon's ankles, don't you Buster? Nicest ankles in the world, aren't they? Biteable and snappable and nippable.'

Everyone laughed. 'You're an idiot, Bets,' said Pip. 'Are we going up to the camp, Fatty? We shall have to find out who lets out those caravans, and see if we can get the name and the address of the woman who was in the one with the twin babies.'

'Yes. That's the first thing to do,' said Fatty. 'Everyone got bikes?'

Everyone had. Buster was put into Fatty's basket, and off they all went, ringing their bells loudly at every corner, just in *case* Mr Goon was coming round in the opposite direction!

Ern, Sid, and Perce were most delighted to see them. Fatty looked at Sid, but when he saw his jaws working rhythmically as usual, he snorted.

'Not much good asking Sid anything,' he said. 'We'll only be able to get "ar" out of him. Sid, if you get many more spots, you'll be clapped into hospital and treated for measles!'

Sid looked alarmed. Ern spoke to him sternly.

'Go and spit it out. You're a disgrace to the Goon family.'

'Ar,' said Sid, looking really pathetic.

'He can't spit it out,' said Perce. 'It's not the kind of toffee for that. Try some, Ern, and see.'

'No thanks,' said Ern. 'Well, count Sid out of this, Fatty. He's hopeless.'

'Yes – but he's quite important,' said Fatty. 'Well, he'll just have to nod or shake his head, that's all, when I ask him questions. Sid, come here. Stop chewing and listen. I'm going to ask you some questions. Nod your head for "yes", and shake it for "no". Understand?'

'Ar,' said Sid, and nodded his head so violently that some of the toffee went down the wrong way and he choked.

Ern thumped him on his back till his eyes almost fell out of his head. At last, Sid was ready again, and listening.

'Sid, do you know the woman's name?' asked Fatty.

'Ar,' said Sid and shook his head.

'Did you ever see her speaking to the prince?' asked Fatty.

'Ar,' said Sid and shook his head again.

'Don't keep saying "ar" like that,' said Fatty, aggravated. 'It's positively maddening. Just shake or nod, that's all. Did you see where the woman went when she wheeled away the pram?'

Sid shook his head dumbly.

'Do you know ANYTHING about her except that she had twins and lived in that caravan?' asked Fatty, despairing of ever getting anything out of Sid at all. Sid's head was well and truly shaken again.

'A man in a lorry came to get the things out of the caravan,' volunteered Perce, unexpectedly.

'What was the name on the lorry?' asked Fatty at once.

'Wasn't none,' said Perce.

'Well, a fat lot of help you and Sid are,' said Fatty in disgust. 'You don't know a thing – not even the name of the woman!'

'Oogleby-oogleby,' said Sid suddenly, looking excited. Everyone looked at him.

'Now what does *that* mean?' wondered Fatty. 'Say it again, Sid – if you can.'

'Ooogleby-oogleby-*oogle*by!' said Sid valiantly, going red in the face.

'He's talking foreign, isn't he?' said Ern, with a

laugh at his own wit. 'Here, Sid – write it down. And mind your spelling!'

Sid took Ern's pencil and wrote painfully on a page of his notebook. Everyone crowded round to see what he had written.

'MARGE and BURT', Sid had printed.

'Marge and Burt,' said Larry. 'Does he mean margarine and butter?'

Everyone looked at Sid. He shook his head at once, and then pretended to hold something in his arms and rock it.

'*Now* what's he doing?' wondered Bets. 'Rock-a-bye baby – Sid, you're dippy!'

'Oh, *I* know, he's pretending to be holding two babies – he must have written the names of the twins!' cried Daisy. Sid nodded, pleased.

'Ar,' he said. 'Oooogly-oogly.'

'Well, I don't know if it's going to help us to know the name of those twin babies,' said Fatty, looking extremely doubtful, 'but I suppose it might. Thanks for your help, Sid – such as it is. Ern, see he doesn't eat any more toffee. Honestly, it's disgraceful.'

'What are we going to do now?' asked Pip.

'We're going to find out who lets these caravans and see if they'll tell us the name and address of the woman who took that one,' said Fatty, waving towards the empty caravan nearby. 'Come on. We'll go now.'

'Can I come too?' asked Ern eagerly. But Fatty said no, he'd no bicycle. He didn't want Ern, Sid, and Perce trailing round them all morning. It would look rather conspicuous to go about in such a large company.

'All right,' said Ern, mournfully. 'Spitty.'

Bets looked at him in delight. 'Oh, *Ern*! I'd forgotten you used to say that, when you meant "It's a pity". Fatty – don't you remember how he used to run all his words together when we knew him before?'

'Yes,' said Fatty, getting on his bike. 'Swunderful! Smarvellous! Smazing!'

15. AN INTERESTING MORNING

And now began a morning of real investigation for the Find-Outers. They rode off down to Marlow, where the agent lived who let the caravans. Fatty had copied down the address from a big notice in the field.

'CARAVANS TO LET,' it said, 'APPLY CARAVANS LTD, TIP HILL, MARLOW.'

They found Tip Hill, which was a little road leading up a hill. Halfway up, in a small field, stood a caravan marked, 'CARAVANS LTD. Apply here for caravans to be let.'

'Here we are,' said Fatty. 'Who would like to do this part?'

'Oh you, Fatty,' said Bets. 'You always do this sort of thing so well. We'll come and listen.'

'No, you won't,' said Fatty. 'I'm not going to have a lot of giggling and nudging going on behind me. If I do this, I do it alone.'

'All right – do it alone,' said Pip.

Fatty went in through the little gate and up to the door of the caravan. He knocked on it.

It opened, and a youth stood there with a cigarette hanging from the side of his mouth.

'Hello!' he said. 'What you want?'

'I'm anxious to find the person who rented one of the caravans next to the school camp field,' said Fatty. 'Could you tell me her name and address, please? I'd be most obliged. She left before I could ask her what I wanted to know.'

'My word – aren't we la-di-da!' said the youth. 'Think I've got time to hunt up names and addresses of your caravan friends, Mister?'

Fatty glanced at the side of the caravan. He saw the name of the owners there in small letters. 'Reg and Bert Williams.' He guessed the youth was just an employee.

'Oh well, if you haven't time, I'll go and ask Mr Reginald Williams,' said Fatty, at a venture. He turned away.

The youth almost fell down the caravan steps. ''Ere, you! Why didn't you tell me you knew Mr Reg?' he called. 'I'll get the address if you wait half a tick.'

Fatty grinned. It was nice to bring that lazy little monkey to heel! 'Very well. But make haste,' said Fatty.

The youth made haste. Fatty thought that Mr Reg, whoever he was, must be a pretty terrifying person if he could shake up a fellow like this merely at the mention of his name! The youth hunted through a large file and produced a list of the caravans up on the hill by the school camp field.

'Now which caravan is it?' he asked. Fatty had noted the name, of course.

'It was called "River View",' he said. 'Quite a small one.'

The youth ran his finger down a list. 'Ah – here we are – Mrs Storm, 24 Harris Road, Maidenbridge. That's not far from here – 'bout two miles.'

'Thanks,' said Fatty, and wrote it down.

'You going to see Mr Reg?' asked the youth, anxiously, as Fatty turned to go.

'No,' said Fatty, much to the youth's relief. He went out to where the others were waiting.

'Got it!' he said, and showed them the name and address. 'Mrs Storm, 24 Harris Road,

Maidenbridge. About two miles from here. Come on – let's get going.'

Feeling rather excited, the five rode off to Maidenbridge. Had Mrs Storm got the prince? Would she tell them anything at all?

They came into Maidenbridge, and asked for Harris Road. It turned out to be a narrow, rather dirty little street, set with houses in a terrace.

They arrived at number 24. It was even dirtier than the rest in the street. Ragged curtains hung at the windows, and the front door badly wanted a lick of paint.

'I'll tackle this too,' said Fatty. 'You ride to the end of the street and wait for me. It looks funny for so many of us to be standing at the front door.'

Obediently, the others rode off. Fatty stood his bicycle at the kerb and knocked. An untidy woman, her hair half down her back, opened it. She said nothing, but just looked at Fatty, waiting.

'Oh – er, excuse me,' said Fatty, 'are you Mrs Storm?'

'No. I'm not,' said the woman. 'You've come to the wrong house. She don't live here.'

This was a bit of a shock.

'Has she left then?' asked Fatty.

'She never did live here, far as I know,' said the woman. 'I've bin here seventeen years, with my husband and my old Ma – I don't know no Mrs Storm. Not even in this street, I don't.'

'How strange,' said Fatty. He looked at the paper with the name and address on. 'Look – it says Mrs Storm, 24 Harris Road, Maidenbridge.'

'Well, that's this house all right – but there's no Mrs Storm,' said the woman. 'There's no other Harris Road but this, either. Why don't you go to the post office? They'll tell you where she lives.'

'Oh thanks, I will,' said Fatty, 'sorry to have troubled you for nothing.' He departed on his bike, puzzled. He joined the others, told them of his failure, and then they all cycled to the post office.

'I want to find someone's address here please,' said Fatty, who was certainly in command that morning. 'I've been given the wrong address, I'm afraid. Could you tell me where a Mrs Storm lives?'

The clerk got out a directory and pushed it across to Fatty. 'There you are,' he said. 'You'll find all the Storms there, hail, thunder, and snow!'

'Ha, ha, joke,' said Fatty politely. He took the

directory and looked for STORM. Ah – there were three Storms in Maidenbridge.

'Lady Louisa Storm,' he read out to the others. 'Old Manor Gate. No, that can't be her. She wouldn't rent a caravan. Here's another – Miss Emily Storm.'

'She wouldn't have twin babies, she's a Miss,' said Bets. 'We want a Mrs.'

'Mrs Rene Storm,' read out Fatty. 'Caldwell House. Well, that seems to be the only one that's likely.'

They left the post office. Fatty turned to Daisy. 'Now *you* can do this bit, Daisy,' he said. 'You must find out if Mrs Rene Storm has twin children.'

'Oh, I *can't*,' said Daisy, in a fright. 'I simply can't walk up and say, "Have you got twin babies?" She would think I was mad.'

'So you would be if you did it like that,' said Fatty. 'Now – you're a Find-Outer, and you haven't had much practice lately. You think of a good way of finding out what we want to know, and go and do it. We'll sit in some ice cream shop and wait for you.'

Poor Daisy! She racked her brains frantically as they all rode along to find Caldwell House. It was a little house set in a pretty garden. Round the corner was a café, and here Fatty and the others sat down to have ice creams and wait for Daisy.

'A nice big double ice cream for you, Daisy, when you come back with your news,' said Fatty. 'In fact, a treble one if this Mrs Storm is the right one. Remember, we only want to know if she has twin babies.'

Daisy rode off. She rode round a block of houses two or three times, trying to think how she could find out what Fatty wanted to know. And then an idea came to her. How simple after all!

She rode to Caldwell House, and put her bicycle by the fence. She walked up to the front door and rang the bell. A little wizened maid opened the door. She looked about ninety, Daisy thought!

'Please excuse me if I've come to the wrong house,' said Daisy, with her nicest smile, 'but I'm looking for a Mrs Storm who has twin babies. Is this the right house?'

'Dear me, no,' said the little maid. 'My Mrs Storm is eighty-three, and she's a great-grandmother. She has never had twins, neither have her children, nor her grandchildren. No twins in the family at all. I'm sorry.'

'So am I,' said Daisy, not quite knowing what else to say. 'Er – well, thank you very much. I'm afraid she's not the Mrs Storm I'm looking for.'

She escaped thankfully and rode quickly to the ice cream shop. The others were pleased to see her come in beaming.

'Is it the right woman?' said Fatty.

'No, I'm afraid not,' said Daisy. 'I'm only beaming because I managed it all right. This Mrs Storm is eighty-three and a great-grandmother – and there aren't any twins in her family at all.'

'Gosh,' said Fatty dolefully. 'Now we're at a dead end then. That wretched caravan woman gave a false name and address. We might have guessed that! We can go hunting the country up and down all we like, but we'll never find a Mrs Storm with twins!'

'Where's my ice cream?' said Daisy.

'Oh, *sorry* Daisy!' said Fatty. 'What am I thinking of! Waitress, a double ice cream please – and another single one all round.'

As they ate their ice creams, they discussed what

to do next. 'Could we possibly look about for twin babies?' asked Bets.

'It's *possible*,' said Fatty, 'but I feel it would take rather a time, looking for all the twin babies there are in this district!'

'How would you set about it, Bets?' asked Pip, eyeing her teasingly. 'Put up a notice – "Wanted, twin babies. Apply Bets Hilton".'

'Don't be silly,' said Bets. 'Anyway, have you got a better idea? What *can* we do next? We haven't a single clue now.'

'Only my button,' said Pip, and pulled out his blue and gold button. He put it down on the table. They all looked at it. It really was a beautiful button.

'Beautiful, but completely useless as a clue,' said Fatty. 'Still, keep it if it pleases you, Pip. If you happen to see a pair of blue and gold pyjamas on a washing line with one button missing, you'll be lucky!'

'Well, that's an idea,' said Pip. 'I shall look at all the lines of washing I see. You just never know!' He put the button back into his pocket.

'What about baby shows?' said Daisy, suddenly.

'We might see twin babies there, and find out where they live.'

'*Baby* shows!' said Pip, in disgust. 'Well, if anyone's going to snoop round baby shows, it won't be me. You and Bets can do that.'

Bets gave a little exclamation, and pointed dramatically to a notice on the wall of the shop. They all looked, and jumped in surprise.

'BABY SHOW,' said the notice. 'At Tiplington Fair, 4 September. Special prizes for TWINS.'

16. OFF TO TIPLINGTON FAIR

'Funny coincidence,' said Fatty, with a laugh. 'Now, let's see – where's Tiplington? Other side of Peterswood, isn't it?'

'You don't *really* think there's anything in Bets' idea, do you?' said Pip, in surprise.

'Well, there's just a chance, I suppose,' said Fatty. 'Bets has had good ideas before. Will you and Daisy go over, Bets?'

'Yes,' said Bets promptly and Daisy nodded. 'Why can't you boys come too? After all, it's a Fair. It should be quite fun. We could take Ern too – he might recognise the twins if they *did* happen to be there!'

'Right. We will take Ern,' said Fatty. 'But not Sid or Perce.'

'I don't mind Perce so much, but I can't bear Sid,' said Bets. 'He's so *chewy*.'

'I can think of a lot more things I don't like about Sid,' said Larry.

'So can we all. Let's change the subject,' said Fatty, feeling in his pocket for money. 'Now, how many ice creams did we have?'

'Oh, Fatty – don't pay for all of them,' said Daisy. 'Larry and I have got plenty of pocket money today.'

'My treat,' said Fatty. 'I'm your chief, don't forget, and I expect to pay some of the – er – expenses we run up.'

'Thank you, Fatty,' said Bets. 'You're a very, very *nice* chief.'

'The fourth of September is tomorrow,' said Daisy. 'I hope it's fine. Who'll tell Ern?'

'Pip,' said Fatty, promptly. 'He hasn't done much in the way of jobs today – you and Bets and I seem to have done most. Pip's turn to do something.'

'All right,' said Pip. 'But if Sid comes "arring" at me I shall throw him into the river.'

'Do,' said Fatty. 'It will probably make him swallow all his toffee at once and get rid of it!'

They decided to meet the next day at Larry's, and all go over to Tiplington together on their bicycles. Ern was to join them at Larry's too, and Larry would borrow an old bicycle for him.

'Two o'clock,' said Fatty. 'And tell Ern to wash

his face and brush his hair and clean his nails, and put on a clean shirt if he's got one. My orders.'

Ern took these orders in good part. Nothing that Fatty said could ever annoy him. 'He's the cat's whiskers,' he told Pip. 'A genius, he is. Right, I'll be there, all spruced up, like. What are we going over to the Fair for? Anything cooking?'

'Might be,' said Pip. 'Don't be late, Ern.'

'I won't,' said Ern. 'Slong!'

It took Pip a moment or two to realise what 'Slong' meant. Of course – 'So long!' Where did Ern learn to mix up his words like that? 'Slong!' What a word!

Ern set off joyfully to go to Larry's the next day. He had difficulty in stopping Sid and Perce from coming too. 'Well, you can't,' he said. 'Look at your hair – and your faces – and your nails – and your shirts! Disgraceful! You can't go out in company like that.'

'Well, it's the first time you've brushed your hair or cleaned your nails,' grumbled Perce.

Ern walked down to the river and took the little ferry boat across. He then walked to Larry's. On the way, to his horror, he met his uncle. Mr Goon advanced on him, even redder in the face than usual, with the heat.

'Ha! Young Ern again!' he began. 'And where may *you* be off to, I'd like to know! You got any more fairy tales for me about princes in prams with twin babies?'

'No, Uncle. No,' said Ern. 'I'm afraid I can't wait. I mustn't be late.'

'Where you going?' asked Mr Goon, and a heavy hand descended on Ern's shoulder.

'To Larry's,' said Ern. Mr Goon looked him over carefully. 'You're all dressed up – hair brushed and all,' he said. 'What are you up to?'

'Nothing, I tell you, Uncle,' said poor Ern. 'We're all going over to Tiplington Fair, that's all.'

'What – that potty little Fair?' said Mr Goon in astonishment. 'What are you going there for? Has that big boy got something up his sleeve?'

'He might have,' said Ern, wriggling free with a sudden movement. 'He's brainy, he is. He believes the things I tell him, see? Not like you! We're investigating hard, we are! And for all you know, we're on to something!'

He ran down the road, leaving Mr Goon

breathing hard. Now, did Ern mean what he said? Was there something going on at Tiplington that he, Mr Goon, ought to know about? Why was that toad of a boy taking all his lot over there?

Mr Goon went home, brooding over the matter. He suddenly made up his mind. He would go to Tiplington too! He ought to keep an eye on that boy anyway. You never knew when he would smell out something.

Mr Goon wheeled out his bicycle and mounted it with a sigh. He didn't like bicycling in hot weather. He was sure it wasn't good for him. But duty called, and off he went.

He started before the others, who had waited for Ern, and had had an ice cream each in the sweetshop in the village before they set off. Buster was in Fatty's bicycle basket as usual, his tongue hanging out contentedly. He was at his very happiest when he was with all the Find-Outers together.

Ern was happy too. He had forgotten about his uncle. He was proud to be with the Find-Outers, and proud that they wanted him. He beamed all over his plain, plump face.

'Slovely,' he kept saying. 'Streat.'

'What do you mean – Street?' asked Daisy, trying to work it out.

'He means, it's a treat,' said Bets laughing.

'SwatIsaid,' said Ern, puzzled.

'Swatesaid,' chorussed everyone in delight.

They rode off down the lanes to Tiplington. After about a mile, they caught sight of a familiar figure in dark blue, labouring at the pedals of his bicycle.

'It's Mr Goon!' said Pip, in surprise. 'Surely *he's* not going to Tiplington too! Don't say he's visiting the baby show as well! Ern! Did you tell him we were going to the Fair?'

Ern went red. 'Well, yes, I did,' he said. 'Didn't I ought to have? I didn't think it mattered?'

'You certainly ought not to have,' said Fatty, annoyed. 'Now we shall have him shadowing us all the time. Still, he probably won't want to do the important thing – look at the twins in the baby show! You'll have to take Ern into the baby show with you, Bets and Daisy – in case you want him to identify any twins.'

'Coo,' said Ern. 'Let me off the baby show! I'm not Sid. I'd run a mile from a baby show!'

'Well, you won't run a mile from this one,' said Daisy, firmly. 'If there are any likely twins, I shall fetch you in, Ern. So don't dare to disappear.'

'Sawful,' said poor Ern. 'Really, sawful this.'

'Sagonizing,' said Fatty. 'Sunendurable.'

'You talking foreign again?' asked Ern, with interest.

'Not more than you are,' said Fatty. 'Now – altogether – pass Mr Goon and ring your bells hard. Bark, Buster, bark. And everyone yell, "Good afternoon, how are you!" '

And so, to Mr Goon's alarm, annoyance and discomfort, six children rode noisily past him with bells ringing, Buster barking madly, and everyone shouting loudly.

'GOOD AFTERNOON, HOW ARE YOU!'

Mr Goon nearly went into the ditch. He scowled after the backs of the six speeding cyclists. He was almost exhausted already. Still, Tiplington wasn't really very far away now. He pedalled on manfully. If there was anything at Tiplington that he'd got to know about, he must certainly be there. There was no knowing what that pest of a boy was up to.

The Fair was certainly not much of a show. It was in a small field. In one big tent was a flower show, a fruit show, a jam show, and a baby show. There were the usual sideshows – a small roundabout, swings, and a hoopla stall. A fortune-teller sat in a very small tent, reading people's hands for them, telling them of great good fortune to come, voyages across the sea, and all the usual fairy tales.

Apparently the Fair was to last three days, but the local flower, fruit and baby shows only this one afternoon. 'Lucky we saw the notice yesterday,' said Bets, as they paid the entrance fee at the gate. Buster was let in for nothing, but Fatty put him on a lead.

'When does the baby show begin?' wondered Daisy. 'Look – there's a notice on that tent. And here are some babies arriving too. Goodness, they look hot, poor things!'

Prams of all types were wheeled in. The four boys wandered off, but Daisy and Bets stood watching the babies being wheeled into the tent.

Daisy clutched Bets' arm suddenly. 'Look, a double pram – and another. Twins!' she said. 'Where's Ern? We shall never know if the babies are the ones that were up in the caravan.'

Ern had completely disappeared. He had been having a lovely time on the roundabout, riding on an elephant, when he had caught sight of his uncle wheeling his bicycle in at the gate, red in the face, dripping with perspiration, and panting loudly. Ern didn't like the look of him.

So, when the roundabout stopped, he slipped quietly off the elephant and made his way to the tent of the fortune-teller. He hid behind it, watching Mr Goon's movements. Ern was not going to have any more to do with his uncle than he could help.

Daisy and Bets disappeared into the big tent, for the baby show was about to begin. How annoying of Ern to vanish! Still, perhaps he would come along soon.

'Four sets of twins!' said Bets. 'Oh, aren't these babies fat? I don't think I like them quite so fat. And they look so hot and miserable. I'm sure this tent is too hot for them.'

'Come and look at the twins,' said Daisy. 'I say, we don't really *need* Ern, you know, because we know the twins' names – Marge and Bert!'

'Oh *yes*,' said Bets, remembering. 'We can just

ask the mothers their names. That's easy.'

The first twins, one big and one small, and quite unalike, were called Ron and Mike, their proud mother informed the two girls.

'No good,' whispered Bets. 'They're boys. We want a girl and a boy.'

The next two were both girls – Edie and Glad, so their mother said. The next pair were again boys, exactly alike, down to the same spot on their chins. Alf and Reg.

'Here's a girl *and* a boy,' said Bets. 'What are their names?'

'The girl's Margery, and the boy's Robert,' said the mother proudly. 'Big for their age, aren't they?'

Bets and Daisy thought they were far too big, far too fat, and far too hot. But their names were right – or almost right!

'Margery and Robert!' said Bets to Daisy in a low voice. 'Marge and Bert. Where's Ern? We'll have to ask him to come and look at them.'

They made their way out of the tent in great excitement and, at last, ran into Ern behind the fortune-teller's tent, where he was still hiding. They pulled him over to the tent.

'You simply *must* tell us if we've found the right babies!' said Bets, and got a sudden punch in the back from Daisy! She gave a squeal. 'Why did you . . .' she began.

And then she saw why! Mr Goon was standing just at the entrance to the tent. He was most interested in what Bets had just said to Ern! Oho! So they *had* got Ern over for something special, thought Mr Goon.

Ern went into the tent, followed by Mr Goon. 'Oh blow,' said Bets. 'Ern, it's the babies at the far end of the row. Just walk quietly by them and tell us if they're the ones we're looking for. Nod your head if it is. Shake it, if not. And look out for Mr Goon!'

Ern walked down the row of babies. Bets and Daisy watched anxiously. Would he shake or nod his head? But, most annoyingly, Ern did neither!

17. THE BABY SHOW

Mr Goon also walked down the row of babies. The little things were terrified of his big, blue-clad figure and his brilliant red face. They began to cry.

'Yow!' they wailed. 'Wow-yow-wow!' Mr Goon scowled at them. He didn't like babies. Also, he was worried. He was remembering Ern's extraordinary tale of the prince being smuggled away in a pram with twin babies. And, lo and behold – here was a row of twin babies! Did Fatty really believe that tale then? *Could* there be something in it?

Mr Goon decided to take quite a lot of notice of the twins. He stood gazing at them. He prodded one or two. He watched Ern walk by them all, looking carefully. He watched him go out of the back flap of the tent, and then he followed him.

The mothers were thankful to see him go. 'What's he want to come in here for, frightening our babies?' said one mother. 'He's set them all off crying with his scowls and his prods!'

Ern had found Bets and Daisy.

'Ern, *why* didn't you either nod or shake your head?' asked Bets crossly. 'You said you would. We *must* know if they are the twins or not. Are they?'

'I don't know,' said Ern, helplessly. 'All those babies in there look alike to me. I couldn't tell t'other from which. Oh, Bets – I'm sorry. They're as like as peas.'

'How *annoying*,' said Daisy. 'Especially as those two are called Margery and Robert.'

'Of course, Bert might be short for Albert or Hubert, as well as Robert,' said Bets. 'We don't know that Bert, the twin Sid knew, was short for *Robert*.'

'*I* know!' said Daisy, suddenly. 'Let's look for the pram that Margery and Robert came in. Ern could surely recognise *that* if it was the one.'

'Oh yes,' said Ern, confidently. 'It was – let me see – was it dark blue, or dark green?'

The two girls stared at him, exasperated. 'You're perfectly hopeless!' said Daisy. 'What good are you to us, I'd like to know! You never notice a thing!'

Ern looked very woebegone indeed. Mr Goon emerged from the tent at that moment and, to the girls' great annoyance, Ern at once made off at top speed! Now they would lose him all over again!

'Ern! Come back and look at the prams!' shouted Bets. Mr Goon pricked up his ears again. Prams! Prams! There *was* something up this afternoon. Those kids *were* investigating something, drat them!

Bets and Daisy gave up on Ern. They wandered over to where the prams were neatly set out in a row, empty of their babies. There were two enormous double prams, one fairly big one, altered to take two children, and any amount of ordinary single prams.

'Perhaps we'd better wait about here for Ern,' said Bets, bored. 'He'll come back sooner or later, I suppose. I wonder what the three boys are doing. Oh, do look at Mr Goon. He's interested in prams too!'

Mr Goon was now examining the prams. Could he find anything in them that would help him? He didn't think so. He considered each pram carefully, much to the amazement of a mother coming out to get something for her baby.

'Thinking of buying a pram?' she asked him.

Mr Goon didn't deign to reply. He wandered off

in search of Ern.

Soon the mothers began to bring out their babies to their prams. They had all been judged, and 'Margery and Robert' had a big rosette each, with 'First Prize, Twins' on it.

'Oh!' said Bets, starting forward. 'Did they get first prize! How lovely! Let me carry one for you. I like babies.'

'Well, perhaps you'd just bring me my pram,' panted the mother, loaded down with her two heavy children. 'It's over there.'

'Which one?' asked Bets.

'That one,' said the mother, nodding at a rather shabby small pram. It was a single pram! Bets had been sure she would have had a double one – what a disappointment. Margery and Robert *couldn't* be the twins they were looking for, after all! Ern and Sid had been quite certain that the pram belonging to the twins in the caravan was a double one.

She brought the little single pram over. 'There now, Madge,' said the mother, settling the little girl at one end, and then putting the boy at the other. 'Now now, Robbie – don't you start yelling.

Haven't you got first prize? Laugh then, laugh!'

Daisy looked at Bets. Madge and Robbie – not Marge and Bert! That settled it. They were not the twins and this was not the mother. All this way over to the Fair for nothing!

'Come along, Bets – let's have a bit of fun now,' said Daisy. 'We've done our investigation – and like all our investigations so far, it's just come to nothing. I don't believe we'll ever find anything out in this mystery!'

They went off to the swingboats. Then they had a try at the hoopla and Bets got a ring round a little red vase, much to her delight.

Then up came Fatty. 'Bets! Daisy! Any good? Were they the twins? What did Ern say?'

'Oh Fatty, such a disappointment! There were twins there whose names were Margery and Robert and we felt sure they were the ones!' said Daisy. 'But they weren't. They were called Madge and Robbie! Ern wasn't a bit of good. He had a look at all the twins, but he said they were as like as peas, and he wouldn't know if they were the caravan twins or not!'

'And, anyway, they have a single pram not a

double one,' said Bets. 'We've come all this way for nothing.'

'Oh no, you haven't,' said Fatty, pulling her over to the roundabout. 'Come on, choose your animal and I'll pay the roundabout boy twice as much as usual to go on twice as long. You can have the longest ride you've ever had in your life!'

Bets chose a lion and the roundabout boy set the roundabout going at top speed, so that Bets and the others yelled in glee! He let them have such a long ride that everyone stared in surprise.

'That was fun,' said Bets, getting off her lion and feeling rather wobbly about the legs. 'Goodness, I still feel as if I'm going round and round.'

Fatty suddenly saw Mr Goon in the distance. He grinned. He went over to the roundabout boy, and had a long talk with him. The boy laughed and nodded. Fatty slid some money into his hand and walked away.

'What have you been up to, Fatty?' said Daisy. 'You've got a wicked look on your face.'

'I've just been arranging for Mr Goon to have a nice long ride,' said Fatty. 'Giving him a real treat, I am! Just you watch!'

Mr Goon had given up searching for the elusive Ern. In any case, he would never find him because Ern was lying hidden under a caravan belonging to one of the Fair people at the end of the field. So now Mr Goon was wandering over to where he saw Fatty, Bets, and Daisy. They were joined by Larry and Pip, who had been unlucky at hoopla, and had no money left.

'Watch,' said Fatty under his breath. They all watched, though not quite certain what they were supposed to watch. The roundabout boy and another one got up on the roundabout as Mr Goon drew near. They began to shout at one another.

Everyone turned to see what was happening. 'You give it to me, I say!' yelled one boy. 'Or I'll box your ears!'

'Shan't!' shouted the other boy, and lunged out at the first boy. Down he went on the platform of the roundabout, and rolled about, yelling loudly.

'Don't worry, Bets. It's all pretence,' said Fatty, grinning. 'Now watch what happens!'

Mr Goon heard all the rumpus, of course. He pulled down his tunic, put his helmet quite straight, and walked ponderously over to the roundabout.

'Hey, you boys! What's the matter there! Behave yourselves!'

'Help, help! He's on top of me!' yelled one of the boys. 'Help! Fetch the police!'

Mr Goon mounted the platform of the roundabout, watched by scores of people, looking very impressive indeed. 'Now what's all this?' he began, and then he suddenly clutched at a nearby tiger.

The roundabout boy had slid off the platform and had started the roundabout! Round it went and round, the music sounding very loud indeed in Mr Goon's startled ears. He nearly fell over. He clasped his arms round the neck of the tiger and yelled ferociously.

'Stop this thing! Stop it, I say!'

But nobody heard him through the din of the strident music! The roundabout went faster and faster, it simply WHIZZED round, till Mr Goon's figure could no longer be clearly seen. Fatty began to laugh. The others rolled about, squealing with joy. Everyone yelled. Mr Goon was not popular in Tiplington!

The roundabout slowed down at last. Mr Goon

still clutched the neck of the tiger. He dared not let go. Poor Mr Goon – the world still went round for him, and the tiger seemed his only friend!

18. PIP'S DISCOVERY

'I have a sort of feeling we'd better go,' said Fatty. 'Where's Ern? Oh, there he is. Good thing he saw a bit of the fun!'

Ern came over to them, grinning. 'I say, look at Uncle on the roundabout. He's still got hold of the tiger. Was it an accident, Fatty?'

'Not quite,' said Fatty, with a rich chuckle. 'Do come on, everyone. Mr Goon won't be fit to follow us on his bike for quite a while. He'll probably want to go round in circles for ages.'

He winked at the roundabout boy, who winked back. Mr Goon straightened up, unwrapped one arm cautiously from the tiger, and took a step away from it. But the world immediately seemed to swim round him again, and he embraced the tiger more lovingly than ever.

'If I look any more, I shall die of laughing,' said Larry. 'I've already got a frightful stitch in my side.

I have never laughed so much in my life. Dear old Mr Goon – I feel quite fond of him for making me laugh so much. How he will ever get off that roundabout, I don't know!'

Fatty had to shove everyone along. They all so badly wanted to see Mr Goon get off the roundabout and walk unsteadily over the field. The roundabout boy was now shouting at him. 'Sorry, sir! Quite an accident. Won't charge you a penny, sir! Free ride for the police force!'

Mr Goon decided not to deal with that roundabout boy just yet. His words seemed to swim round in his head. He didn't want to argue with anyone just then. He held the tiger still more tightly, and shut his eyes to see if the world would steady itself again.

The Find-Outers and Ern found their bicycles and mounted them. 'Come down this path,' said Ern. 'It's a shorter way to the road. I saw it when I was hiding under the caravan.'

So they took Ern's path that led across the field, past the caravans, and out into a lane that went straight to the road.

And it was when they were cycling slowly past

the caravans that Pip suddenly saw something that made him almost wobble off his bicycle!

Clothes lines stretched here and there, hung with the washing belonging to the Fair people. Pip glanced at it idly as he went by. He saw a blouse there, a blue blouse made of rather common material – but it wasn't the blouse that gave him such a surprise – it was the buttons on it!

'Gosh!' said Pip. 'Surely they're the same as the button I've got in my pocket – the button that came off Prince Bongawah's pyjamas!'

He took the button out of his pocket and went over to the clothes line. He compared it with the buttons on the blouse. They were exactly the same – blue and gold, very fine indeed.

Pip glanced at the nearby caravan. It was bright green with yellow wheels. He would remember that all right. He rode fast after Fatty, almost upsetting the others on the narrow path as he passed them.

'Stop it, Pip!' cried Bets angrily, as he almost brushed her pedal. 'What's the hurry?'

Pip caught Fatty up at last. 'Fatty! Quick. Stop a minute, I've got something important to say!'

Fatty stopped in surprise. He got off his bicycle and waited by the little gate that led into the lane. 'Wheel your bike out under those trees, so that we can't be seen talking,' panted Pip.

Everyone was soon standing under the trees, surprised and puzzled. 'What is it, Pip?' said Fatty. 'What's up all of a sudden?'

'You know this button that came off Prince Bongawah's pyjamas?' said Pip, producing it. 'Well, Fatty, when we passed those clothes lines I saw a blouse hanging on one – and it had buttons *exactly* like these all down the front! And you must admit they're very fine and very unusual buttons!'

'Gosh!' said Fatty, startled by this remarkable statement of Pips'.

He took a quick look at the button and then walked back the way he had come, wheeling his bicycle. 'I must check up,' he said in a low voice as he went. 'Wait for me. I'll pretend to be looking for something I've dropped in the grass.'

He went along with bent head until he came to the clothes line. He spotted the blouse at once. He went right up to it, still pretending to look for something on the ground – and then took a good look at the blouse which was now almost touching his nose.

He came back quickly. 'Pip's right,' he said, his voice sounding excited. 'This is very important. We thought we'd wasted the afternoon, coming after twin babies – and so we had from that point of view – but we're on to something much better!'

'What?' asked Bets, thrilled.

'Well, obviously those buttons are off the prince's pyjamas,' said Fatty. 'And quite obviously, also, the pyjamas have been destroyed in case they might be recognised. But whoever destroyed them couldn't bear to part with the lovely buttons – and put them on that blouse, thinking they would never be noticed!'

'They wouldn't have been if Pip hadn't found that button, and noticed the washing!' said Bets. 'Oh Pip, you *are* clever!'

'Let's think,' said Fatty. 'Let's think quickly. What does it mean? It means that the prince is probably somewhere here – hiding – or being hidden. Probably in that caravan near the washing line. We'll have to try and find out.'

'We can't very well stop now,' said Pip.

'Mummy said Bets and I were to be back by six – and we won't be if we don't hurry.'

'*I'll* stop behind,' said Fatty, making up his mind quickly. 'No, I won't. I'll go back, change into some disguise, and come back here. I'll get into talk with the Fair people and see if I can pick something up. Yes, that's the best thing to do. One of us must certainly make enquiries quickly.'

'Let me stop too,' said Ern.

'Certainly not,' said Fatty. 'You go back with the others, Ern. Go on. Do as you're told. I'm chief here. Let's ride back quickly because it will take me a little time to put on a disguise.'

'What will you be, Fatty?' asked Bets, excited, as they all cycled quickly down the lane, Ern looking a little sulky.

'A pedlar,' said Fatty. 'Selling something. I can easily get into talk with the Fair people then. They'll think I'm one of them. I simply must find out if there has been a new boy added to their company just lately!'

'Good gracious! From being quite unsolvable, this mystery has jumped almost to an end!' said Bets.

'Don't you believe it,' said Fatty grimly. 'There's

more in this than meets the eye. It's not as straightforward as it looks. There's something funny about it!'

This all sounded extremely exciting. The six of them rode along in silence, each thinking the same tumultuous thoughts. What would Fatty find out? Would he discover the prince that evening? What was the 'something funny' he meant?

They got home in good time. Fatty went straight down to his shed. He knew exactly what disguise he would wear. It was one he had worn before, and he felt it was just right.

It was an ordinary schoolboy who went into the little shed – but an ordinary schoolboy didn't come out! No, a pedlar crept out, a dirty-looking creature with long earrings in his ears, a cloth cap pulled down over his face, a brilliant red scarf round his neck, and protruding teeth. Fatty was in disguise!

Dirty flannel trousers clothed his legs and old gym shoes were on his feet. He wore a red belt and a dirty yellow jersey. On his back was a pack. It held bottles of all kinds marked 'Cold Cures', 'Cures for Warts', 'Lotion for Chilblains', and all kinds of weird concoctions that Fatty had invented himself for his pedlar's pack!

He grinned as he crept up the path. His protruding teeth showed, ugly and white. He had fixed a fine false set over his own, made of plastic. Fatty was going investigating – and nobody in the world would have guessed he was anything but a dirty little travelling tinker or pedlar!

He cycled off, back to Tiplington. That was clever of Pip to spot those buttons. Very clever. It put the mystery back on the map, so to speak. Fatty thought rapidly over his plan.

I'll go to the Fair field. I'll sit down and get into talk with the roundabout boy or someone. I'll find out who lives in that green and yellow caravan, and pretend I know the people there – and perhaps get the roundabout boy to take me over and introduce me. Then I'll see who's in the caravan and have as good a snoop round as I can. Well, I hope the plan will work!

He was soon back at the Fair. There were more people now because it was evening. The roundabout was swinging round bravely. The swingboats were flying high. There was a babble of talk and laughter everywhere.

Now then, thought Fatty, carefully hiding his bicycle in the middle of a thick bush. Now then! Once more into the breach, dear friend – and see what's what!

He sauntered in to the field. No one asked him for entrance money because he looked exactly like one of the Fair folk themselves. Fatty looked round. The roundabout boy was there at his place. Should he have a word with him? No, he was too busy. What about the hoopla boy? No, he was busy too. Fatty strolled along, keeping his eyes open.

He came to the swingboats. The man looking after them was standing holding his arm as if in pain. Fatty walked up. 'What's up, mate? Hurt yourself?'

'One of these swingboats came back and knocked my elbow,' said the man. 'Look after them for me for a few minutes, will you, while I go and get something for it?'

'Right,' said Fatty, and looked after the swingboats faithfully till the man came back, his arm neatly bandaged.

'Thanks,' he said. 'You with us, or have you just come along?'

'Just come along,' said Fatty. 'Heard that maybe someone I knew was here. Thought I'd give them a call-in.'

'Name of what?' said the man.

'I can't remember the name for the moment,' said Fatty, taking off his cap and scratching his head hard. He screwed up his face. 'Let me see now – Barlow, Harlow, no, that wasn't it.'

'What line were they in?' said the man.

'Ah wait – something's coming back to me!' said Fatty. 'They had a green caravan with yellow wheels. Anyone here in a caravan like that, mate?'

'Oh yes, the Tallerys,' said the man, taking some money for a ride in his swings. 'Those who you mean? They've got that green and yellow caravan over there!'

'That's right – the Tallerys!' exclaimed Fatty. 'How did I come to forget the name! Are they all still there, mate?'

'Well, there's old Mum, and there's Mrs Tallery, and there's a nephew, Rollo,' said the man. 'That's all. Old Man Tallery's not there. He's on a job.'

'Ah,' said Fatty, as if he knew quite well what the job was. 'Well, I feel uncomfortable at going along to them if Old Man Tallery's not there. The others might not remember me.'

'I'll take you along, chum,' said the obliging swingboat man. 'Say, what's your name?'

'Smith,' said Fatty quickly, remembering that many gypsies were called Smith. 'Just Jack Smith.'

'You wait till this lot's finished their swings and I'll take you over,' said the man. 'Maybe they aren't there though. I did see Old Mum and Mrs Tallery going off this afternoon.'

'Well, I'd be glad if you'd take me across,' said Fatty. 'You can tell them I knew Old Man Tallery!'

19. ROLLO TALKS A LOT

The swingboat man took Fatty across to the yellow and green caravan. An old woman was outside, sitting in a sagging wicker chair that creaked under her great weight.

She was calling loudly to someone, 'Rollo! Drat the boy, where is he? I'll give him such a hiding when I get hold of him!'

'Hello, Old Mum,' said the swingboat man, coming up. 'That scamp of a Rollo gone again? I'll give him a clip on the ear if I see him, and send him over to you. He's the laziest young 'un I ever did see in my life.'

'He is that,' grumbled Old Mum. 'His aunt's gone down to the town, and he was told to clean the windows of the caravan. They're that dirty I can't see to knit inside!'

She peered at Fatty. 'Who's this? I don't know him. Do you want Old Man Tallery? He's not here. Won't be back for a few days.'

'Oh, I'm sorry,' said Fatty. 'I wanted to see him.'

'Friend of his,' the swingboat man explained to Old Mum. 'Name of Jack Smith.' He turned to Fatty. 'You sit and talk to the old lady a bit. She'll love that! What have you got in your pack? Anything to interest her? I'm going back to my swings.'

Fatty opened his pack and displayed his bottles and tins. Old Mum took one look at them and laughed a wheezy laugh.

'Ho ho! That's your line, is it? Coloured water and coloured powders! My dad was in the same line and very paying it was too. Shut your pack up, lad, I've no use for them things. I'm too old and too spry to be caught by such tricks!'

'I wasn't going to sell you any, Old Mum, or try to,' said Fatty, in a voice very like Ern's. 'When did you say Mrs Tallery would be back?'

'Oh, I never know how long she'll be,' said Old Mum crossly. 'Here, there, and everywhere she is. Here today, gone tomorrow – leaves me alone for days on end, she do. Off she went a few days ago, never said where – and back she comes without a word.'

Fatty pricked up his ears. Could Mrs Tallery be the woman in the caravan – the woman with the babies?

'Let me see now,' said Fatty, 'how many children has she got?'

'She and Old Man Tallery never did have children,' said Old Mum. 'Nary a one. That's why they took on Rollo, though gracious knows why they wanted to pick on him, the little pest. But his Ma's got eleven kids besides him, so she was glad to get rid of him.'

'Oh, of course,' said Fatty, quite as if he knew all about it! He was about to ask a few more questions when the swingboat man came up again, leading a boy by the ear.

'Here's Rollo, Old Mum,' he said. 'Shall I set him to work cleaning the windows, or shall I put him across my knee and give him a hiding first?'

'No!' yelled Rollo, squirming about. 'I'll do the windows, you big beast!'

The swingboat man shook him, laughed, and went off again. Fatty looked at the angry boy. He wasn't very big, about Pip's size, and the scowl on his face made him very ugly and unpleasant. Old

185

Mum began to scold him soundly, the words pouring out of her mouth in an endless stream. The boy made a rude face at her.

He then went to get a pail of water and a cloth, presumably to clean the very dirty windows. Old Mum heaved herself up to go into the caravan.

'I'm chilly,' she said. 'Just keep an eye on that boy, will you? Give me a call if he stops his work!'

Fatty helped the old woman into the caravan. She seemed surprised at his help. 'Well, 'tisn't often my son, Old Man Tallery, has friends like you!' she said. 'First time I've known one of them help me up the steps!'

She disappeared into the smelly, dirty caravan. The boy sulkily sloshed water over the windows, and made them so wet and smeary that Fatty thought they were worse than ever!

He sat and waited till the boy had finished. Rollo emptied the water, threw the cloth under the caravan, and made a face at Fatty.

'Here,' said Fatty, taking some money out of his pocket. 'I'm hungry. Go and buy something with this, bring it back, and we'll share it. Skip along!'

'Right,' said the boy, looking less sulky. He took the money and went. Soon he was back with two meat pies, gingerbeer, and four enormous jam tarts. He sat down by Fatty.

'You a friend of Old Mum's?' he said. 'Misery guts she is. I like my aunt better. No nonsense about *her*.'

'You've got plenty of brothers and sisters, haven't you?' said Fatty, eating the pie. He didn't like it at all. It was dry and musty.

'Yes. Eleven,' said Rollo. 'The youngest are twins. Always yelling they are.'

'*Twins*?' said Fatty at once. 'How old are they?'

'Don't know,' said Rollo. 'Just babies. They came to stay with my aunt when my mum was ill.'

'What, here?' said Fatty, munching away. 'I shouldn't have thought there was room for all of you in the caravan.'

'They was only here for a day,' said Rollo. 'Then my aunt got a caravan up on the school camp field and had them there.'

Fatty went on munching solidly, but his eyes suddenly gleamed in his dirty face. Aha! He was on the track now all right! So the aunt was the woman in the caravan – and Rollo's twin brother and sister were the twins in the pram!

'Let me see – Marge and Bert are the twins, aren't they?' said Fatty. Rollo nodded.

'That's right. You know the family all right, don't you! There's Alf, George, Reenie, Pam, Doris, Millie, Reg, Bob, Doreen – and Marge and Bert.'

'And you're the one they chucked out, are you?' said Fatty, gazing at the jam tarts and wondering if he dared to tackle one.

'Ere! Oo said I was chucked out!' said Rollo indignantly. 'What do you suppose Old Man Tallery picked *me* out of the lot for? *I'll* tell you. Because I can act, and because I've got brains, and because I'm jolly useful to him!'

'I bet you're nothing but a nuisance to him, a dirty little rascal like you!' said Fatty, trying to rouse Rollo into telling him a lot more things. Rollo rose to the bait at once. He scowled.

'I'm going to tell you something, Mister,' he said to Fatty. 'I can act anything, I can. I can be a boy leading a blind fellow – that's one way Old Man Tallery and me get money – and I can be a nice kid going shopping with my aunt, and slipping things up my sleeve when Aunt's talking to the shop girl – and I can even be a *prince*!'

Fatty jumped. A prince! Now what did he mean by that? Fatty turned and stared at the gypsy boy, who looked back impudently at him.

'Ah, that made you stare!' said Rollo, triumphantly. 'I bet you don't believe it, Mister.'

'No, I don't,' said Fatty, hoping to lead the boy on and on. His mind was in a whirl. A prince? What did it all mean?

'I thought you wouldn't believe me!' said Rollo. 'Well, I've said too much. I'd better not say any more.'

'That's because you've got nothing to say,' said Fatty promptly. 'You're making up a lot of tales and you know it. Prince, my foot! Dirty little rascal like you a prince! What do you take me for?'

The boy glared at him. Then he looked all round as if afraid that someone might overhear. 'Look here,' he said, 'do you remember the fuss in the papers about that prince being kidnapped. Prince Bonga-Bonga or something. Well, I was him!'

'Go and tell that fairy tale to the twins!' said Fatty scornfully, but inwardly very excited. 'There's a *real* Prince Bongawah, who belongs to a real kingdom called Tetarua – I've seen photographs of him.'

'Well, I tell you, I was him!' persisted the boy, angry that Fatty wouldn't believe him.

'Really? Well maybe you'll tell me how you were kidnapped then, and how you got away, and were taken here,' said Fatty sarcastically.

'Easy,' said the boy. 'I wasn't kidnapped. I just had to stay a few days at the camp, see, and pretend to be the prince and just talk gibberish – and then on a certain night, I had to creep through the hedge, find my aunt's caravan, and hide there. You'll never guess how I got away though!'

Fatty thought he could make a very good guess indeed, but he pretended to be quite bewildered.

'My word – this is a tale and a half!' he said. 'Do you really mean to say you did all that? Well then – how *did* you get away?'

'My aunt took the bottom boards out of the twins' double pram, and I curled myself up in the space there,' said Rollo, grinning. 'And she sat the twins down on top of me. They didn't half yell!'

'And then she wheeled you back here,' said

Fatty, as if overcome with admiration. 'Well, you are a one, Rollo! I didn't believe a word at first, but I do now. You're a marvel!'

Rollo beamed at once at this unexpected praise. He leaned over to Fatty and whispered, 'I could tell you something else if I wanted to!' he said. 'I could tell you where the *real* prince is! The coppers would give a lot to know what *I* know, I can tell you! Not half they wouldn't!'

20. FATTY RIDES HOME

Fatty was so astonished that he couldn't say a word! He gazed speechlessly at Rollo and Rollo grinned delightedly.

'You're a friend of my uncle's, Old Man Tallery, so it won't matter telling *you* all this,' he said, suddenly struck by the fact that he had been telling a lot of secrets! 'But don't you let on to him that I told you.'

'No, I won't,' said Fatty. 'He's not here, anyway. Where is he?'

'Well, he thinks I don't know, but I do,' said Rollo. 'He's down in Raylingham Marshes. I heard him and Joe talking when they didn't know I was near.'

'Is that where the prince is – the real prince?' asked Fatty.

Rollo grew suddenly cautious. 'Here, I'm telling you too much. What's come over me! You just forget what I said about the prince, see? I don't know where he is.'

'You said you did just now,' said Fatty.

'Well, maybe I do and maybe I don't,' said Rollo. 'Anyway I'm not telling *you*.'

'Right,' said Fatty. 'Why should I want to know anyway? But what beats me is why you had to dress up as the prince and then run away and make people think you were kidnapped. It doesn't make sense to me.'

'Well, it ought to,' said Rollo rudely. 'But maybe your brains want a bit of polishing up.'

'Go on!' said Fatty. 'You and your cheek! I don't say I'm as bright as you are, by a long chalk. I could think a hundred years and not see why all this was done!'

'Well, you look here,' said Rollo, really enjoying himself. 'There's a prince that someone wants to get rid of, see – so that he won't have the throne. Got that?'

'Yes,' said Fatty, humbly.

'But it would be jolly difficult to kidnap him and get him out of the country before his disappearance was discovered, wouldn't it?' said

Rollo. 'So all that happened was that when he was sent down to the school camps by car, the chauffeur stopped at an arranged place, the prince was whisked away in another car – and I popped into the first car, all dressed up posh like the prince!'

Fatty suddenly saw light. So *that* was the how and the why and the where! Someone wanted the prince out of the way, but didn't want the kidnapping to be discovered till he had had time to get the boy away somewhere – and with the chauffeur in the plot, it was easy! Exchange boys on the journey down, let the second boy stay a few days in the camp and behave as if he were the real prince – and then creep away to his convenient aunt, and disappear with the twins in the double pram! No one would ever think the woman had anything to do with the second 'kidnapping', which, to all intents and purposes, was the first and only kidnapping. Nobody guessed about the genuine kidnapping!

'What a plan!' said Fatty, in a tone of deepest admiration. 'Old Man Tallery is a whole lot cleverer than I thought he was. My word, next time I meet him, I'll ask him to let me come in on his next job.

There must be a lot of money in these things.'

'There is,' said Rollo, boasting hard now. 'I reckon he'll clear hundreds of pounds. I'm going to have some myself, for my part in playing the prince.'

'My word – you'll be rich!' said Fatty. 'How did you like being a prince? Didn't you ever forget your part?'

'No. It was easy,' said Rollo. 'My colouring is as dark as the prince's, and we was both little fellows, and I didn't have to speak any English – only nonsense. But when one of the big fellows – the ones who arranged all this, you know – came down to see how I was getting on and insisted on having the state umbrella up, I didn't like that. I felt a fool. All the boys yelled at me.'

'Did you enjoy being a prince?' Fatty asked him.

'Not so bad,' said Rollo. 'I slept in pyjamas for the first time in my life – lovely silk they were, all blue and gold, with buttons to match. My aunt was told to burn the pyjamas as soon as I got here, and she did, in case anyone saw them. But she kept the buttons and sewed them on a blouse. She didn't like throwing those away, they were too good.'

Fatty couldn't help thinking what a good thing

it was that Rollo's aunt had been thrifty over the buttons! If she hadn't sewn them on her blouse, if she hadn't washed it and hung it on the line, Pip would never have spotted the buttons and he, Fatty, would never have got on to the well-hidden trail!

'I suppose Old Man Tallery helped to arrange everything,' said Fatty. 'He's great, isn't he, your uncle?'

'No flies on *him*,' said Rollo proudly. 'He's a card, he is. I quite enjoyed being a prince, but when they wanted me to go swimming, I didn't half kick up a fuss. The way they talked about me not wanting to wash, too. Wash, wash, wash, clean your teeth! Many a time I wanted to talk back at those kids up at camp. I did say a few things in English – but I was a bit afraid of giving myself away if I lost my temper.'

'Of course,' said Fatty. 'Well, you seem to have done very well. I don't believe anyone suspected you weren't the real prince. Are you like him to look at?'

'Near enough,' said Rollo. 'He wasn't anything special to look at and neither am I. I was a bit scared of someone who knew the prince coming down to see me, but nobody did.'

'And you say you know where they took the prince?' said Fatty. 'Haven't they got him away from there yet?'

Rollo became secretive again. 'I'm not telling that,' he said. 'I don't want to be skinned alive by my uncle, see? He doesn't even know I heard where he's gone to.'

Fatty decided that he couldn't find out anything else from Rollo. He knew the whole plot now – very simple, very slickly carried out – the real kidnapping cleverly masked by the false one so that the police were completely bamboozled, not looking for the prince until some days after he had *really* been kidnapped!

Had the real prince been spirited away yet? Would he ever be heard of again? There really was no time to be lost if he was still being kept in hiding. Anything might happen to him at any time!

Raylingham Marshes. If Rollo's uncle, Old Man Tallery, was there, possibly the whole gang were there, and the Prince too. Where were Raylingham

Marshes? Fatty decided to look them up immediately he got home.

He got up to go. It was getting dark and only the Fair people were now left on the field. He had missed dinner – thank goodness his parents were out, and wouldn't know he wasn't there. 'Well, so long!' he said to Rollo. 'I must be going.'

'Aren't you going to wait and see my aunt?' said Rollo, who had taken quite a fancy to Fatty. 'What did you say your name was?'

'Jack Smith,' said Fatty. 'No, I can't wait. Give her all the best from me, and say I'll look in another time. She may not remember me, of course.'

She jolly well won't! thought Fatty to himself, as he went to find his bicycle and ride home. Blow! I haven't got a lamp. I forgot I might be home after dark. Hope I don't get caught by old Mr Goon!

Fatty rode off quickly. His mind was working at top speed. What a plot! No wonder it had seemed such a peculiar mystery – there had been two kidnappings, but only one – the false one – was made known!

Raylingham Marshes. Was there a house in the

marshes? Was the prince hidden there? Had Rollo got the name right, or was he doing a little make-up on his own? He was talkative and boastful and conceited – some of what he said might quite well not be true. Fatty rode along so lost in thought that he was in Peterswood before he realised it.

He rode cautiously down the road. As he had no lights he was extra careful – but suddenly a dark figure stepped out from behind a tree, and said sharply, 'Here you! Stop! What you doing, riding without a light? Don't you know it's against the law?'

Mr Goon! thought Fatty. Just my luck! He got off his bicycle, debating what to say and do.

Goon flashed his lantern at him, and saw what appeared to be a dirty tramp with a pack. Mr Goon was suspicious at once.

'This your bike?' he asked sharply.

'Might be!' said the pedlar, insolently.

'Now you come-alonga me,' began Mr Goon, 'and give a proper account of yourself. Riding without a . . .'

'Here hold my bike for a minute while I do up my shoe,' said the pedlar, and shoved the bicycle at Goon. He had to catch it to save it from falling on top of him – and while he stood there holding it, Fatty was off like a streak of lightning!

'Oho! So that's the way of things, is it?' said Goon. 'He's stolen this bike, that's what he's done.'

Goon mounted the bicycle and rode after the running figure. But it darted off down a path where cyclists were not allowed to ride, and Goon was beaten! He had no wish to ride a bicycle without lights down a path where cycling was forbidden! Ten to one, if he did, that big boy would appear from somewhere and see him! Goon got off and wheeled it carefully back to his house. The bicycle seemed somehow vaguely familiar to him. He took it into his hall and had a good look at it. Then he got out his notebook and wrote down a full description.

'Full-size. Make – Atlas. Colour – black with red line. Basket in front. No front lamp. In good condition.'

Then he wrote a full description of the man he had seen with it.

'Tramp. Cloth cap pulled down over face. Red scarf. Dirty jersey. Dirty flannel trousers. Earrings. Rude and insolent. I had to force him to give up bicycle, which I guessed was stolen. After a terrific struggle I got it, and the man ran off, scared.'

Just as he finished writing all this, the telephone rang and made him jump. He picked up the receiver.

'Police here,' he said.

'Oh, Mr Goon, is that you?' came Fatty's voice at the other end. '*So* sorry to bother you – but I have to report to you that my bike's been stolen. It's gone. Not in the shed. Vanished. I'm afraid you'll never find it or the thief, but I thought I'd better report it.'

'Details of your bike please,' said Goon, in a most official voice.

'Right,' said Fatty. 'Full-size, of course. It's an Atlas, a rather nice one in good condition. It's black with a red line, and there's a basket in front. And . . .'

Goon cleared his throat and spoke pompously. 'I have it here, Frederick. I stopped a tramp with it fifteen minutes ago. Very nasty fellow he was too. Most insolent. Didn't want to give up the bike at all when I challenged him.'

'How did you get it then?' asked Fatty in an awed voice.

'Well, I struggled with him,' said Goon letting his imagination go. 'It was a bit of a struggle, you know – but I got it from him. He was so scared that he ran for his life. I brought the bike here. You can come round for it, if you like.'

'My word, you've done some pretty quick work, Mr Goon!' said Fatty admiringly. Mr Goon stood up very straight. Aha – it wasn't often that boy said things like that to him.

'I don't let the grass grow under my feet,' said Mr Goon, with dignity. 'Well, you'll be along in a minute or two, Frederick, I suppose?'

'Give me ten minutes, and I'll be there!' said Fatty cheerfully, and rang off with a click.

21. MR GOON HAS A BAD TIME

Fatty arrived in ten minutes, looking spruce and clean. He had just had time to get out of his disguise and clean himself up. He had given himself one minute to laugh very loudly indeed at Goon's story of the tramp and the fight he had had.

Goon opened the door. He was still pompous. 'There's your bike,' he said, waving to where it stood in the hall. 'Can't beat the police, you know, Frederick.'

'Well, I must say it was pretty smart work, Mr Goon,' said Fatty so admiringly that Mr Goon told the story of the tramp all over again, adding a few more trimmings.

'Mr Goon, I'm much obliged to you,' said Fatty earnestly. 'And, in return, I must pass on a bit of news. We've discovered a bit more about the kidnapping – I know Ern told you about the prince hiding in a pram under the babies, didn't he? Well, we've found out now that that wasn't the real prince. It was a gypsy boy. The real prince is, we *think*, somewhere in Raylingham Marshes.'

Mr Goon's face slowly grew thunderous as Fatty reeled all this off. 'Now look here,' he said, 'why don't you think up some better tale? How many more princes are you going to tell me about?'

'I'm not fooling you, Mr Goon,' said Fatty. 'I said I'd help you this time, and I'm trying to. But you make it very difficult.'

'So do you,' said Mr Goon. 'What with your dressing up as foreigners, and talking foreign, and then telling Ern to tell me about princes in prams with babies, and now you say he was a gypsy, and you want me to go gallivanting off to Raylingham Marshes after another prince. Not me!'

'I don't want you to do any gallivanting at all,' said Fatty. 'All you've got to do is to ring up the Chief Inspector and tell him everything. He'll tell you what to do.'

'Look here,' said Mr Goon, beginning to turn his usual purple, 'didn't I ring up and tell the Chief all about Princess Bongawee, the Prince's sister – and it was all made up on your part to make me look small? Oh, you needn't shake your head, I know it was! Then you wanted me to tell him another idiotic story – and now this. Well, I shan't!'

'You'd better,' said Fatty. 'Or shall I? If I do, I'll get all the credit again, you know.'

'Don't you do any telephoning either,' snapped Mr Goon. 'Can't you keep out of this? I'm in charge of this case, I tell you. Interfering with the law! That's what you do all the time. You're a toad of a boy, a . . .'

'Shush shush, Mr Goon,' said Fatty, beginning to wheel his bicycle out of the hall. 'Naughty naughty! Mustn't lose temper.'

He wheeled his bicycle to the front gate and mounted it. Then he called back, 'Oh, I say, I forgot to ask you something, Mr Goon. Did that tramp you fought with do up his shoe after all?'

And, without waiting for an answer, Fatty rode chuckling down the road. Mr Goon stared after him in the darkness. He was puzzled. How did that boy know that the tramp had said he wanted to do up his shoe? Certainly Mr Goon had mentioned no such thing. Then *how* did Fatty know it?

Light suddenly dawned on Mr Goon. He

staggered into his sitting-room and sat down heavily in his chair. He put his head in his hands and groaned. The tramp had been Fatty! He had taken his bike away – and patted himself on the back when Fatty had reported it gone – and given it back to him without so much as mentioning the missing front lamp!

Why, oh why, had he made up such a wonderful story? How Fatty must have laughed up his sleeve! Mr Goon spent half an hour thinking of all the horrid things he would like to do to Fatty but, alas, he knew he would never, ever get the chance to do them. Fatty could look after himself too well!

The telephone rang and Mr Goon jumped. He picked up the receiver fiercely. If it was that boy again, he'd tell him what he thought of him!

But it wasn't. It was a message from the Chief Inspector, delivered shortly by another constable.

'That PC Goon? Message from the Chief. A report has come through from one of our men to say it is now thought that the boy at the camp was not the real prince – but someone masquerading as him. Photographs shown to boys on the field have not been recognised as the boy who was with them as the prince. The Chief says, have you had any inkling of this – if so, please send in your report.'

Mr Goon gaped. He didn't know *what* to say. Why, it seemed as if the message Ern had delivered to him from Fatty might have been correct after all then – not a fairy tale. That story about the prince getting away in the pram – and now Fatty's tale about it being a gypsy boy after all! Was it all true?

'PC Goon? Are you still there?' said the voice at the other end impatiently. 'Did you hear me?'

'Yes – oh yes,' panted Goon, feeling suddenly as if he had been running a long way. 'Thanks. Interesting report. I'll – er – think about it – and send in mine shortly.'

'Right. Goodnight,' said the voice, and the telephone clicked off.

For the second time that night, Goon sank down into his chair and put his head in his hands, groaning. Why hadn't he told the Chief all that Ern had told him? Now someone else had got the information, and got in before him. Goon began seriously to wonder if he owned as good brains as he thought himself to have.

First I ring up and tell the Chief about that

dressing-up and Princess Bongawee, which was nonsense, he thought. And then I *don't* tell him about the prince going off in the pram with those babies. That's why those kids were over at the Fair, no doubt about that – trying to trace the babies and their mother.

He sat and brooded for some time. Then he thought of the last thing Fatty had said to him – that he thought the *real* prince was in Raylingham Marshes.

Was that true? Did he really think so? Dare he ring up and tell the Chief that – or would it turn out that there wasn't such a place or something?

Mr Goon began to get into a state. He paced up and down. He clutched his head. He groaned. He'd lose his job over this if he didn't do something special now!

He got down a police map of the district. He looked up Raylingham Marshes. Yes, there was such a place. But was it just marshes and nothing else? Suppose there wasn't even a house there?

'There's only one thing to do,' said Mr Goon, making up his mind. 'I must go and see this place. Let's see, what's the time? There seems to be a station within a mile or two of the place. Is there a train I can catch?'

He looked up the timetable. There was a train, the very last train, in three-quarters of an hour. Mr Goon began to do things in a great hurry.

He took off his uniform and put on ordinary clothes. It wouldn't do to go snooping round a hide out in police uniform. He dragged on a pair of enormous, grey flannel trousers, added a grey jersey with a bright yellow border at the neck and bottom, and a cap. He put on a tweed coat, rather baggy, and then looked at himself in the glass.

Nobody would guess I was a police officer! he thought. Talk about disguises! Well, I can do a bit of that too. I'm just a hiker now, that's all. I'll put a few things in a kit-bag to make meself seem real.

He caught the train by the skin of his teeth. It arrived on time at the station near to Raylingham Marshes – Raylingham Station – a sleepy little place with one man who was porter, ticket clerk and everything.

He seemed surprised to see Mr Goon on the last train. 'Did you want to get out here, mate?' he asked.

'I did,' said Mr Goon. 'Er, I'm a hiker, you see.

I'm – er – seeing the countryside.'

'Well, don't you go hiking over them marshes in the dark,' said the porter, puzzled.

'Are there any houses in the marshes?' asked Goon.

'Not many,' said the porter. 'Two, that's all. One's a farm, on high ground, and the other's a big house. Belongs to foreigners, so people says.'

Aha! thought Goon. That's the house I want. I'll get there somehow, and snoop round. I might find the prince. I might even rescue him.

Wonderful pictures of himself carrying the prince on his back across dangerous marshes came into Mr Goon's mind. Even more wonderful pictures came after that – photographs of himself and the prince in the papers. Headlines – 'Brave Constable Rescues Kidnapped Prince'.

Mr Goon left the dimly-lit station and stepped out into the darkness. There was a lane outside the exit. He would follow that – very, very cautiously. It must lead somewhere!

The porter watched him go. 'Funny chap,' he said to himself. 'Mad as a hatter! Hiking over the marshes in the middle of the night. The police ought to be told about *him* – ought to keep an eye on him, they ought!'

But nobody kept an eye on the brave and valiant Mr Goon. He was quite, quite alone.

22. DISAPPEARANCE OF MR. GOON

Fatty had done nothing that night except to look up the map to find Raylingham Marshes, if there *was* such a place. There was, as Goon had already found. Fatty examined the map closely.

I believe I could get into the marshes from this bit of high ground here, he thought. There's a path or something marked there. Two buildings marked as well – one at one end of the marsh, one in the middle. There's a station too. Well, I certainly won't go by train – much too conspicuous.

He decided to go to bed and sleep on the whole idea. He would tell the others about it in the morning. He was much too tired to do any more 'gallivanting' about that night and, anyway, he wasn't going to lose himself in unknown marshes in pitch darkness!

The telephone rang while he was eating his breakfast next morning. The maid answered it and came into the room.

'Frederick, it's for you,' she said. 'Chief Inspector Jenks on the telephone.'

Fatty jumped. His father looked at him at once. 'You haven't been getting into any trouble, Frederick, I hope,' he said.

'I don't think so,' said Fatty and disappeared hurriedly into the hall, wondering what in the world the Chief wanted at this time of the morning.

'Frederick? Is that you?' came the Chief's crisp voice. 'Listen – Goon's disappeared. Do you know anything about it?'

'Gosh!' said Fatty, startled. 'No, I don't, sir. I saw him late last night. He – er – found my bicycle for me after I had – er – reported it gone. He certainly didn't make me think he was going to disappear.'

'Well, he has,' said the Chief Inspector, sounding annoyed. 'He didn't answer his telephone this morning and when I sent a man over, he reported that Goon was gone – not in his uniform either.'

'Don't say *he's* disappeared in his pyjamas too – like the prince!' said Fatty, still more startled.

'I don't know,' said the Chief. 'Nobody would kidnap Goon, I should imagine – not out of his own house! It's most extraordinary. You are sure you don't know anything about it, Frederick? You usually seem to know a good deal more than most people.'

'No, sir. Honestly, I didn't know he had gone – or was meaning to go anywhere,' said Fatty, very puzzled. 'I can't make it out.'

'Well, I can't stop for more now,' said the Chief. 'Ring me if you have any ideas. Good-bye.'

And before Fatty could ask him or tell him anything more, the telephone went dead. Fatty stared down at it. He was most surprised at this news.

Goon disappeared! He must have gone after I left him. It was dark then, and he was in his uniform. He must have undressed. Gosh, don't say he's gone in his pyjamas too – this is all very peculiar! Fatty quite forgot that he hadn't finished his breakfast, and went out to get his bicycle to ride round to Larry's.

Larry was surprised to see him so early. 'No time to talk much now,' said Fatty. 'Come round to Pip's, you and Daisy. There's a lot of news.'

There certainly was! The others drank in all Fatty had to say about the boy in the caravan the night before, and what he had told Fatty.

'So you see, Sid was quite right when he told us about the boy who was hiding in the pram,' said Fatty. 'And now we know why he hid – and why he pretended to be the prince, and everything.'

'But we don't know where he's been hidden – the real prince, I mean,' said Pip.

'Well, I may even know that,' said Fatty, and he told them what the boy had said. 'He said his uncle, Old Man Tallery, was in Raylingham Marshes,' he went on, 'and as he was mixed up in the kidnapping, and produced his nephew, Rollo, to impersonate the real prince, it's very likely that the prince is there too. There's probably a good hide out there, in those marshes.'

'You did awfully well last night,' said Pip. 'What time did you get back?'

'Late-ish, in the dark,' said Fatty. 'And I hadn't a lamp on my bike – and what do you think! I was caught by Mr Goon!'

'Gracious!' said Bets, alarmed. 'Did he go round and complain to your parents?'

'Of course not. He didn't know it was me. You forget, I was disguised as a tramp,' grinned Fatty, and then told them how Mr Goon had taken his bicycle and how he, Fatty, had got it back again. The others roared with laughter.

'No one will *ever* get the better of you, Fatty,' said Daisy, with the utmost conviction. 'Any more news? What a lot you've got.'

'Yes. I've kept the spiciest bit till last,' said Fatty. 'Mr Goon has disappeared! Nowhere to be found this morning, so the Chief Inspector says – and, he's left his uniform behind. Where, oh where, can he be?'

Nobody knew. They were all astounded at this last bit of news. 'Another spot of kidnapping, do you think?' asked Larry.

'I don't know *what* to think,' said Fatty. 'He certainly didn't appear to have any plans for going anywhere last night when I went to fetch my bike.'

'Of course, if you'd mentioned Raylingham Marshes to him, I would have thought he might be there,' said Bets. 'Just to get in before *you*, Fatty. But he wouldn't know, of course.'

Fatty sat up straight. 'Bets, you're a marvel!' he

said. 'Hit the nail on the head, as usual. I *did* tell him the place, of course – but what with one thing and another, I'd forgotten I'd mentioned it to him. That's where he is!'

'Do you think so *really*?' asked Bets, her face glowing at Fatty's praise.

'Of course,' said Fatty. 'But goodness knows what has happened to him. Got a timetable, Pip? He wouldn't bike all that way, and the buses wouldn't be going at that time of night. But there might be a train.'

There was, of course. 'That's what he did!' said Fatty, jubilantly. 'As soon as I'd gone, he must have got out of his uniform and put on his ordinary clothes and rushed out and caught that train – and gone hunting for the prince in Raylingham Marshes!'

'Without saying a word to anyone!' said Pip. 'What a man!'

'What are *we* going to do about it?' asked Daisy. 'Anything?'

Fatty considered. 'I don't think I'll tell this idea to the Chief. He wouldn't want to send a posse of men searching marshes for Mr Goon unless he was dead certain he was there. We'll go ourselves!'

'What! All of us?' cried Bets, joyfully.

'All of us,' said Fatty.

'And Ern too?' asked Bets, pointing down the drive. Everyone looked and groaned. Ern was coming up the drive – by himself, fortunately.

'Well, I suppose Ern may as well come too,' said Fatty. 'The more the merrier. We'll be a company of kids out walking – looking for unusual marsh flowers and marsh birds.'

'I'll look for the Marsh Goonflower,' said Bets with a giggle. 'And you can look for the Clear-Orf Bird, Pip.'

'Hello, hello, hello!' said Ern, appearing round the hedge. 'How's things? Any news?'

'Yes, a lot,' said Bets. 'But we can't stop to tell you now, Ern.'

'Spitty,' said Ern, looking disappointed. 'What's the hurry?'

'You can come with us if you like and we'll tell you on the way,' said Fatty. 'I hope you haven't got Sid and Perce parked outside the front gate, Ern, because we are *not* going to take them too.'

'I'm alone,' said Ern. 'Perce has gone to buy

some more rope for the tent – it flopped down on us last night. And Sid's gone to buy nougat.'

'*Nougat*!' said everyone astonished. 'But why not toffee?'

'Sid seems to have gone off toffee all of a sudden, like,' said Ern. 'Funny. He's never done that before.'

'Well, nougat is almost worse – so gooey,' said Bets. 'Spitty!'

'Now don't you catch Ern's disease,' said Pip. Ern looked startled.

'What disease?' he asked. 'I haven't got no spots nor anything.'

'We haven't any time to waste,' said Fatty. 'We'll go and buy sandwiches and buns and drinks down in the village. There won't be time to prepare food ourselves. We'll take the bus to the east side of the marshes and then walk.'

They left their bicycles at Pip's and went to buy their food. Soon they were on the bus to Raylingham. Fatty forbade them to talk about anything to do with the mystery. 'Someone might be on the bus that knows something about it,' he said. 'We don't want to give any information away.'

They got out of the bus at the edge of the marshes. They had talked so loudly about flowers and birds all the way that the conductor felt sure they wanted to search the marshes for them.

'You'll be all right so long as you keep to the paths,' he told them. 'See that one there? That leads right to the centre of the marsh. You'll notice other paths going off here and there, but be careful not to choose too narrow a one.'

Off they all went. Was Mr Goon somewhere there? Surely he hadn't fallen into the marsh in the middle of the night, and sunk down and down?

'Till his head's just above the surface of the marsh!' said Bets, with a shiver. 'Only his helmet showing.'

'He's not wearing his helmet,' said Fatty. 'Cheer up. It would take a long, long time for an enormous weight like Mr Goon to sink down and down and down! This is not a terribly *marshy* marsh – not in the middle of summer at any rate!'

But when Pip slipped off the path once, he soon found himself up to the knees in muddy water! He didn't like it at all, and got hastily back on to the path.

'I shan't go looking for Goonflowers just here!' he said. 'I don't feel they'd grow very well!'

23. THINGS BEGIN TO HAPPEN

The marsh was a strange place. It was intensely green and it was also full of the most irritating flies. Ern nearly went mad with them, and the others nearly went mad with Ern's continual slapping and grumbling!

'Look – there's a house or something over there,' said Fatty, suddenly. 'On that high ground, see – where there are trees.'

'How nice to see trees again,' said Daisy. 'I was almost beginning to forget what they looked like. Ern, stop slapping about. You keep making me jump, and it's too hot for that.'

'Let's take this little path,' said Fatty, stopping where a narrow path curved off the main one they were following. 'It seems to go round the back of that copse of trees – it looks almost a wood really – and we could reconnoitre without being seen.'

'What's "reconnoitre",' said Bets at once.

'Spy round – have a snoop,' said Fatty. 'If Raylingham Marshes *is* a hide out for Old Man Tallery and the prince and his kidnappers, we don't want to be caught.'

But they *were* caught! They stole down the narrow little path that skirted the copse, looking carefully down at their feet to make sure they were going to tread safely, when two men rose up from beside a turn in the path. They had been lying behind great tufts of rushes, and couldn't possibly be seen.

The children stopped, alarmed and shocked at such a sudden, silent appearance. The men looked quite ordinary country men, though both had very dark eyes, and a rather odd accent when they spoke.

'Hello,' said Fatty, recovering. 'You startled us!'

'Why do you come through this dangerous marsh?' asked one man. 'It is not fit for children.'

'Oh, we're on a walk,' said Fatty. 'A nature walk. We're not trespassing, you know – this marsh is common ground.'

'But you *are* trespassing,' said the other man, and his dark eyes snapped at Fatty. 'This land belongs to that farm over there. See it?'

'Yes,' said Fatty. 'Well, we're doing no harm.

Now we've come so far, we'll go right on to the other side.'

'Not this way,' said the first man, and he planted himself in Fatty's way. 'You can go back to the main path. I've told you, you are trespassing.'

'What's up that we can't go this way?' said Fatty, impatiently. 'Anyone would think you had something to hide!'

'I say – look!' said Larry suddenly, and he pointed up into the sky. 'What's that? A helicopter, surely! Gosh, it's not coming down into the marsh, is it? It will sink!'

One man said something savage to the other in a foreign language. Both glanced up at the hovering helicopter. Then the first one pushed Fatty firmly back.

'I'm having no nonsense,' he said. 'You'll do as you're told, all you kids. Go back to the main path and, if you're wise, keep away from this marsh, see?'

Fatty stumbled and almost fell into the water on one side of the path. Ern, angry that anyone should have dared to touch his beloved Fatty, gave the man a violent push too. He lost his balance and went headlong into the marsh!

'Shut up, Ern,' said Fatty angrily. 'What's the sense of doing that? We shall only get into trouble! Turn back, all of you, and go to the main path!'

The man who had fallen into the marsh was extremely angry. He clambered out, calling orders to the other man, still in a foreign language.

'You can come along with us,' said the second man to Fatty, grimly. 'You hear? Walk in front of us on this narrow path. We'll show you that we mean what we say when we tell you you are trespassing!'

The helicopter was still hovering over their heads. The men suddenly seemed in a great hurry. They made the children squeeze by them on the narrow path till all of them were in front. Then they made them march ahead quickly.

Nobody said anything. Fatty was thinking hard. That helicopter was about to land. Where? There must be some small landing-place cleared for it somewhere near. Who was it going to take away? The prince? Then he hadn't yet been spirited away. Those men had been on the watch for anyone coming through the marsh that day – something was going on, that was clear.

In silence, the two men hurried the children

along. Bets was frightened and kept close to Fatty. Ern was scared too, and forgot all about slapping at the flies. And all the time, the helicopter hovered about overhead, evidently waiting for some signal to land.

Round a corner, they came into a big farmyard. Pigs were in a sty, and hens wandered about. It looked very homely and countrified all of a sudden. Ducks quacked in a pond, and a horse lifted its head from a trough where it had been drinking, and stared at the little company.

A very big farmhouse lay back from the yard. Its tall chimneys showed that it was old – probably built in Elizabethan times. There was a small door in the wall of the farmhouse not far from them. The men hurried the children over to it, opened it, and shoved them all in, giving them a push if they thought anyone was not quick enough.

Down a long passage – up some narrow, curving stairs, along another passage, with wooden boards that were very old and uneven. The passage was dark, and Bets didn't like it at all. She slipped her hand into Fatty's and he squeezed it hard.

They came to a door. The man in front opened

it. 'In here,' he said, and in they all went. Fatty put his foot in the doorway just as the man was about to shut them in.

'What are you doing this for?' he asked. 'You know you'll get into trouble, don't you? We're only kids out on a walk. What's the mystery?'

'You'll be kept here for a day or two,' said the man. 'There are reasons. You came at an unfortunate time for yourselves. Be sensible and nothing will happen to you.'

He kicked Fatty's foot away suddenly and slammed the door. The six children heard the key turning in the lock. Then they heard the footsteps of the two men as they hurried away down the passage.

Fatty looked desperately round the room. It was small and dark, lined with oak panels. There was one small window, with leaded panes. He ran to it and peered out. A sheer drop to the ground! Nobody could climb out there with safety.

'Fatty! What's all this about?' said Ern, in a frightened voice. 'Sawful!'

'Shall I tell you what I think?' said Fatty, in a low voice. 'I think Prince Bongawah was taken here and hidden, when he was kidnapped from his car. And I think he's been kept prisoner here till arrangements could be made to spirit him away somehow – and that's what that helicopter is arriving for! It will land somewhere here, the prince will be hurried aboard – and nobody will ever hear of him again!'

Bets shivered. 'I don't like you saying that,' she said. 'Fatty, what are we going to do? Do you think they'll hurt us?'

'No,' said Fatty. 'I think we're a nuisance, but I think they really do believe we're only six kids out hiking. They've no idea we're hunting for old Mr Goon, or that we know anything is going on here.'

'But what are we going to *do*?' said Bets again. 'I don't like this place. I want to get out.'

'I can hear the helicopter again,' said Pip. 'It sounds nearer. It must be coming down.'

'Do you suppose Mr Goon is a prisoner too?' said Larry. 'We haven't seen or heard a sign of him. Perhaps he didn't come to Raylingham Marshes after all.'

'Perhaps he didn't,' said Fatty. He went over to the door and tried it. It was locked. He looked at the door. It was old but very stout and strong.

Nobody could possibly break it down!

'Do your trick of getting out through a locked door, Fatty,' said Daisy suddenly. 'There's a good space under the door – I believe you could manage it beautifully.'

'That's just what I was thinking,' said Fatty. 'The only thing is, I need a newspaper – or some big sheet of paper – and I haven't brought a newspaper with me today. Very careless of me!'

'I've got a comic,' said Ern unexpectedly. 'Would that do? What you going to do, Fatty?'

'Get through this locked door,' said Fatty, much to Ern's amazement. Ern fished in his pocket and brought out a crumpled and messy comic, which he handed to Fatty.

'Good work,' said Fatty, pleased. He took the comic and opened out the middle double sheet. He slid it carefully under the door, leaving only a small corner his side. Ern watched, puzzled. How was that going to open a locked door?

Fatty took a small leather case from his pocket and opened it. In it were a number of curious small tools, and a little roll of wire. Fatty took out the wire and straightened it.

He inserted it into the keyhole and began delicately to work at the key. He prodded and pushed and jiggled it – until, suddenly, he gave a sharp push and the key slid out of the keyhole on the other side of the door, and fell with a thud down to the floor.

Ern stared open-mouthed. He couldn't for the life of him make out what Fatty was doing. But the others knew. They had seen Fatty doing his locked door trick before!

'Hope it's fallen onto the paper,' said Fatty, and bent down to draw the sheet of paper back under the bottom of the door. Carefully he pulled it, very carefully. More and more of the comic appeared and, oh joy, at last the key appeared too under the door, on the second half of the double-sheet! There it was, on their side of the door. Fatty had managed to get it!

Ern gasped. His eyes almost fell out of his head. 'Coo – you are a one!' he said to Fatty. 'You're a genius, that's what you are.'

'Be quiet, Ern,' said Fatty. He slid the key into the lock on his side of the door and turned it. The door unlocked. Now they could all go free!

24. FATTY DOES SOME GOOD WORK

'Listen,' said Fatty, in a low voice. 'I don't think we'd all better go out. There's such a crowd of us, we'd be sure to be spotted. What I propose to do is this – get out by myself and have a really good look round. If there's a telephone, I shall immediately use that to get on to the Chief Inspector, and warn him to send men here at once.'

'Ooooh, *yes!*' said Bets, delighted at the idea of rescue.

'Then I shall snoop round to see if I can find the prince – though I'm afraid I won't be in time to stop the helicopter from going off with him, if they mean to take off again at once,' said Fatty.

'What about Mr Goon?' asked Larry. 'Will you look for him?'

'Well, I'll certainly keep a look out for him,' said Fatty. 'But, at the moment, the most important thing is to get in touch with the Chief, and also see if I can hold up the prince's flight. Now all you have to do is to keep quiet and wait. I'll have to lock you in again, I'm afraid, in case someone comes along and finds the door unlocked. But you know how to get out if you want to, Larry, don't you? – so you'll be all right.'

'Suppose someone comes and sees you're not with us?' said Bets, in sudden alarm.

'I don't expect they'll notice,' said Fatty. 'They haven't counted us, I'm sure! Well – slong!'

'So long!' whispered the others. 'Good luck!'

Fatty disappeared down the passage, after carefully locking the door behind him and leaving the key in the lock. He was very cautious. By good chance they had come at a most important moment, and Fatty did not mean to throw his chance away!

The telephone! That was the most essential thing for him to find. Where would it be? Downstairs, of course. In the hall, probably, which would make it very awkward indeed to talk into. He would certainly be heard.

A thought struck Fatty. Sometimes people had a telephone in their bedroom. His mother had, for instance, so that if she happened to have a cold, she could still telephone her orders to the shops, or talk to her friends.

There *might* be one in a bedroom. Fatty decided to look. It would make things so much easier if there were.

He peeped into first one room and then another. Two of them were most luxuriously furnished, considering this was a farmhouse. Fatty stood at the door of one, his sharp eyes looking all round.

Then his face brightened. A telephone in pale green stood beside the big green-covered bed at one side of the room! Gosh! Could he possibly get to it and telephone unheard? He tiptoed across the room, first shutting the door quietly behind him. He took up the whole telephone, and crept under the bed with it, hoping that his voice would be muffled there.

He lifted the receiver and put it to his ear, his heart beating fast. Would the operator answer?

With great relief he heard a voice speaking. 'Number please.'

Fatty gave the number in a low voice. 'It's the Chief Inspector's number,' he said urgently.

'Put me through quickly, will you?'

In under half a minute, another voice spoke. 'Police station here.'

'This is Frederick Trotteville speaking,' said Fatty, keeping his voice low. 'I want the Chief Inspector at once.'

There was a pause. Then came the Chief Inspector's voice and Fatty's heart lifted in joy.

'Frederick? What is it?'

'Listen,' said Fatty. 'I'm at the farmhouse in the middle of Raylingham Marshes. I'm pretty certain the kidnapped prince is here too. There's a helicopter hovering about, and I think maybe we've come at an important moment – when the prince is about to be spirited away. We're prisoners, sir, but I managed to get to a telephone. We're all here, Ern too. Can you send men along?'

There was an astounded silence. Fatty could picture the Chief's astonished face. Then his crisp voice came over the wires. 'Yes. I'll send some. Hang on till we come – and see if you can stop the prince from being taken away! If anyone can, *you* can, Frederick! Good work!'

The telephone went dead. Fatty replaced his

receiver with a sigh of thankfulness. Help would come sooner or later. Now he was free to do a bit of prowling round and see what he could find. If only he could find out where the prince was!

Fatty crawled out cautiously from beneath the bed and replaced the telephone on its little table. He tiptoed to the door. All was quiet. He opened it silently and peered out into the passage. No one was in sight.

Better look for a locked door, thought Fatty. That's the only bright idea I've got at the moment. Let's think now – the farmhouse had two wings to it and I'm in the middle. We must have been locked up in one wing. Maybe the prince is in the other.

He leaned carefully out of a window to have a look at where the other wing of the house stood out. He at once noticed a barred window. Ah, surely that would be the room!

He drew in his head, and made his way down the passage. Was there any way of reaching the other wing except by the stairs and the hall? There might be.

Fatty came to the head of the stairs. Down below he could hear the murmur of voices coming from some room – and then his eye caught sight of something through the landing window.

It was the helicopter! With its vanes whirring, it was slowly descending! Fatty watched it disappear behind a big barn-like building. There must be a landing-place there. He frowned. There was no time to lose now. The prince might be hurried off immediately!

He went to the back of the landing and found a tiny, narrow passage there. Perhaps it ran to the other wing! He followed it carefully and quietly and, as he had thought, it did run to the other wing of the house.

Now to find the locked room with barred windows! thought Fatty jubilantly, and then shrank back in fright as he heard the sound of a door being shut and locked, and a man's voice saying something loudly.

Fatty crouched behind a curtain covering a window, hardly daring to breathe. Footsteps passed by him, and went on to the big landing where the stairs were. When all the sounds had gone, Fatty came out again. He tiptoed quickly along the passage, passed two open doors – and then came to a shut one!

It was locked! But, fortunately, the key had been left in the lock. Fatty turned it, opened the door, and looked in.

A dark-faced boy with a sulky, scowling expression looked up. He was about Pip's size, and in build and colouring was very like Rollo, the gypsy boy.

'Are you Prince Bongawah?' whispered Fatty. The boy nodded, staring in astonishment at this big boy in the doorway.

'Come on then – I've come to save you,' whispered Fatty. 'Hurry up.'

The boy ran to the door and began to jabber in a foreign language.

'Shut up!' said Fatty urgently. 'Do you want to bring everyone up here! Come with me and don't make a sound!'

The boy followed him, suddenly silent. Fatty locked the door behind him. Then, very cautiously indeed, his heart thumping hard against his ribs, he led the boy down the narrow passage, across the landing where the stairs were, and along the passage that led to the other wing.

He unlocked the door where the others were

and pushed the boy inside. Everyone stared in astonishment at Fatty's grinning face and this newcomer, so dark and foreign-looking.

'I've found the prince,' said Fatty jubilantly. 'And I thought the safest place to hide him would be here. He can get into that cupboard. Nobody would dream of looking for him in a room where *we* are supposed to be prisoners!'

'Oh, Fatty – you're full of good ideas!' said Bets. 'Poor prince! He must wonder what's happening.'

The prince spoke beautiful English, and gave them all a little bow.

'I have been a prisoner for many days,' he said. 'I have been unhappy and afraid. You are my friends?'

'Oh yes,' said Bets, warmly. 'Of course we are. You'll be safe now Fatty has got you!'

'I found a telephone and got a message through to the Chief,' said Fatty, unable to stop grinning. 'Golly, what a surprise for this lot when they find the police coming through the marsh and surrounding the farmhouse!'

'Honestly, you're a genius Fatty,' said the admiring Ern. 'I think you ought to be made a Chief Inspector at once, I do!'

'Did you find Mr Goon?' asked Daisy.

Fatty shook his head. 'No – didn't see or hear a sign of him. I'm beginning to wonder if he came here after all.'

'Well, it's a good thing we *thought* he did!' said Bets, 'or we shouldn't have come ourselves! And then we'd have missed all this!'

'Did you see the helicopter come down?' asked Daisy. 'We suddenly saw it landing behind that big barn.'

'Yes, so did . . .' began Fatty, and then stopped speaking and listened. The others listened too.

They could hear shouts – and banging doors and running feet! What was up?

'They've discovered that the prince isn't in his room!' said Fatty, beaming. 'What a shock for them! *Now* there'll be a rumpus! Helicopter all ready to take him off – and no prince to be found! Get into that cupboard, Prince, and keep quiet. Don't make a sound.'

The prince disappeared into the cupboard in double-quick time. Bets shut the door on him. In silence, they listened to the excitement going on elsewhere.

Then footsteps came hurrying down their passage, sounding loudly on the wooden boards. Their door was suddenly flung open.

A swarthy-faced man looked in, his eyes blazing.

'He might be here!' he shouted. 'These kids may have got him with them somehow. Search the room!'

25. A VERY EXCITING FINISH

That was a real shock to everyone! Bets went pale. Only Fatty didn't turn a hair.

'What's up?' he said. 'Who do you think we've got here? You shut six of us up, goodness knows why, and there are six still here!'

The man shouted something at Fatty in such a savage voice that Fatty decided not to say anything more. Three other men crowded into the room and began to look everywhere. In less than a minute the cupboard was opened – and the prince was discovered!

The swarthy-faced man pounced on him and shook him! He screamed something at him in a foreign language and the boy cowered in fright. He was dragged out into the passage. Fatty followed, protesting.

'I say, look here! I say, you know . . .'

The dark-faced man turned on him, his hand

lifted – but before he could strike Fatty, a loud voice shouted down the passage.

'The police! The POLICE are coming! Tom's just seen them coming over the marsh. Someone's split on us!'

Then there was such a babel of noise and excitement that it was impossible for anyone to be heard. Fatty took the opportunity of pulling the prince back into the room, pushing all the other children in too, slipping the key from the outside of the door to the inside – and locking them all in!

As he turned the key, he grinned round at the six frightened faces. 'Cheer up! No one can get at us! We're locked in again but the key's our side all right!'

Bets was crying. 'Oh Fatty, I didn't like that man. Are we safe now? Can they break the door down?'

'They won't bother to try,' said Fatty. 'They'll be too anxious to save their own skins! We can just sit here and listen to the fun – and come out when everything is quiet!'

'There goes the helicopter again!' said Pip suddenly, and sure enough it was rising quickly over the barn. Evidently it had been warned to go.

'But it didn't take *me* with it,' said the prince exultantly, and went off into a stream of what sounded like gibberish to the children.

Not much of the excitement could be seen from the window. Two policemen suddenly appeared and made a rush for the house. One man suddenly ran helter-skelter across the farmyard and disappeared, followed immediately by a burly policeman. Yells and shouts and thumps and crashes could be heard every now and again.

'I'm rather sorry to be out of the fun,' said Fatty regretfully.

'Well, I'm not,' said Ern, who was looking extremely scared. 'Fun! Not my idea of fun. Sterrible!'

After about half an hour, silence reigned. Had all the men been rounded up? Fatty and the others listened. Then they heard a most stentorian voice.

'FREDERICK! WHERE ARE YOU? FREDERICK!'

'The Chief Inspector!' said Fatty thankfully, and ran to unlock the door and open it. He too yelled at the top of his voice.

'HERE, SIR! WE'RE ALL SAFE AND SOUND!'

He turned back to the others. 'Come on,' he

said, 'it must be safe now. Come on, Ern. Your legs too wobbly to walk?'

'Bit,' said poor Ern, staggering after the others.

The Chief Inspector met them all at the top of the stairs. He ran a swift eye over the lot. 'All of you here?' he said. 'Who's this?' He pointed to the prince.

'Prince Bongawah, sir,' said Fatty. 'I got him all right. Did you catch everyone, sir?'

'I think so,' said the Chief Inspector. He pulled the prince to him. 'You all right?' he said. 'They didn't do anything to you, did they?'

'No, sir,' said the prince. 'It was my uncle who kidnapped me. I was . . .'

'We'll hear your story later, son,' said the Chief Inspector. 'Well, Frederick, that was a spot of good work on your part. Though how in the world you managed to smell out this place – and get here on your own – and find the prince – and telephone me in the middle of everything, I don't know! And taking the whole of the Find-Outers with you too – except Buster. Where is he?'

'Had to leave him behind, sir,' said Fatty, regretfully. 'I was afraid he'd fall into the marsh and drown. Pity he's out of the fun though. He does love a scrap.'

'We've got some police cars on the edge of the marsh,' said the Chief Inspector. 'At present, two of them are taking some of the men to the police station but they'll be back soon, and then I'll take you home.'

'Let's have a wander round the place then, sir,' said Fatty. 'It seems odd to have a farm in the middle of a marsh.'

They all went thankfully into the open air. A frightened woman peeped from a doorway at them.

'Who's she?' asked Fatty, surprised.

'The housekeeper', said the Chief Inspector. 'We left her for the present, as someone's got to feed the hens and the pigs and ducks.'

They wandered round the farmyard and then round to the back of the big barn, behind which the helicopter had landed. A big flat space had been cleared there for the landing.

They looked at the cleared space and then walked round it to a group of sheds nearby. They talked cheerfully as they went, all of them feeling very happy to think that everything was over.

A sudden noise made them stop. 'What was that?' said Larry. 'It sounded as if it came from that shed. Is there some animal locked in there? A bull perhaps?'

The noise came again – a loud banging noise, then a series of thuds. The door of the shed shook.

'Better look out,' said the Chief Inspector. 'Sounds rather like a bull in a temper.'

Snorts and groans and yells came next. 'It isn't a bull,' said Fatty. 'Sounds like a mixture of a man and a bull! I'll look and see – through a window, not through a door!'

The window of the shed was very high up. Fatty ran a ladder up against the wall of the shed, went up it and peered through the window. He came down again, grinning.

'Friend of yours, sir,' he said cheerfully, and unbolted the door from the outside. It burst open and out came a big, dirty, perspiring, maddened creature, his fists up, and hair standing on end.

'*Goon*!' said the Chief Inspector, almost falling backwards in his amazement. 'GOON! What on earth – is it *really* you? GOON!'

Yes, it was Mr Goon, and a sorry sight he looked.

246

He was filthy dirty, very angry, and looked as if he had been sitting down in all the messes he could. Straw was caught in his up-standing hair, and he panted like a dog. He stared in astonishment at the little company before him, and quietened down at once when he saw the Chief Inspector.

'Morning, sir,' said poor Goon, trying to flatten down his hair.

'Where did you disappear to without leaving any message as to your whereabouts?' asked the Chief Inspector. 'We've been hunting for you everywhere.'

'I – er – got a hunch that something might be going on here,' said Mr Goon, still sounding out of breath. 'Caught the last train, sir, and somehow I got lost in these here marshes. I found myself sinking down, and I yelled for all I was worth.'

'Oh, Mr Goon! How dreadful for you!' said kind-hearted Bets. 'Did someone rescue you?'

'Rescue me!' snorted Goon, sounding rather like a bull again. 'Yes, they pulled me out all right – and pushed me into that cowshed and bolted me in! What for? They should all be arrested, sir! Mishandling the police! Punching me in the back!'

'Don't worry, we *have* arrested them all,' said

the Chief Inspector. 'You missed that bit of fun.'

'Coo, Uncle – you don't half look funny,' said Ern suddenly, and went off into a loud guffaw. His uncle appeared to see him for the first time.

'ERN! You here too! What you doing here, mixed up in all this?' shouted Goon. 'I'll teach you to laugh at me!'

'Behave yourself, Ern,' said Fatty, severely. He felt sorry for poor Mr Goon. What a hash he had made of everything – and yet he, Fatty, had given him all the information he could!

'It was jolly brainy of Mr Goon to come here, sir, wasn't it?' he said innocently to the Chief Inspector. 'I mean, he got here even before we did. It was just bad luck he fell in the marsh. He might have cleared the whole job up himself if he hadn't done that.'

Mr Goon looked gratified. He also felt suddenly very kindly towards Fatty. He wasn't such a toad of a boy, after all!

The Chief Inspector looked at Fatty. 'Brains are good, courage is excellent, resourcefulness is rare,' he said, 'but generosity crowns everything, Frederick. One of these days, I'll be proud of you!'

Fatty actually blushed. Mr Goon had heard all this, but hadn't understood what the Chief Inspector meant at all. He came towards them, brushing down his clothes.

'So, it's all over, is it?' he said. 'What happened, sir?'

'You'd better go and wash,' said the Chief Inspector, looking at him. 'You've no idea what you look like, Goon. And if you've been shut up all night, you'll be hungry and thirsty. Ask the woman at the farmhouse for something to eat and drink.'

'I could certainly do with something,' said Mr Goon. 'You'll call me when you want me, sir?'

'I will,' said the Chief Inspector. 'We're just waiting for the police cars to come back.'

'Slong, Uncle,' called Ern, but his uncle did not deign to reply. He disappeared in the direction of the farmhouse – an ungainly, peculiar-looking figure, but not at all downcast. Hadn't he got there before that boy, anyhow? And hadn't that boy admitted it? Things weren't so bad after all!

'It was a peculiar sort of mystery this time,' said Bets, hanging on to the Chief Inspector's arm. At first, there didn't seem to be any clues or anything – nothing we could get hold of – and then it suddenly boiled up, and exploded all over us!'

Everyone laughed. 'Bets quite enjoyed this mystery,' said Fatty. 'Didn't you, Bets? I did too.'

'So did I,' said Ern, thoroughly agreeing. 'Not half! Spitty young Sid and Perce weren't in at the finish.'

'Yes. SPITTY!' agreed everyone, chuckling, and the Chief Inspector smiled.

'Well, let me see – when do you have your next holidays?' he said. 'At Christmas time? Right. Here's to the next mystery then – and may it all end as well as this!'